9798643476139

THE LIES SHE TOLD

M A COMLEY

JEAMEL PUBLISHING LIMITED

New York Times and USA Today bestselling author M A Comley
Published by Jeamel Publishing limited
Copyright © 2020 M A Comley
Digital Edition, License Notes

All rights reserved. This book or any portion thereof may not be reproduced, stored in a retrieval system, transmitted in any form or by any means electronic or mechanical, including photocopying, or used in any manner whatsoever without the express written permission of the author, except for the use of brief quotations in a book review or scholarly journal.

This is a work of fiction. Names, characters, places and incidents are a product of the author's imagination or are used fictitiously, and any resemblance to actual persons living or dead, business establishments, events or locales is entirely coincidental.

ALSO BY M A COMLEY

Blind Justice (Novella)

Cruel Justice (Book #1)

Mortal Justice (Novella)

Impeding Justice (Book #2)

Final Justice (Book #3)

Foul Justice (Book #4)

Guaranteed Justice (Book #5)

Ultimate Justice (Book #6)

Virtual Justice (Book #7)

Hostile Justice (Book #8)

Tortured Justice (Book #9)

Rough Justice (Book #10)

Dubious Justice (Book #11)

Calculated Justice (Book #12)

Twisted Justice (Book #13)

Justice at Christmas (Short Story)

Justice at Christmas 2 (novella)

Prime Justice (Book #14)

Heroic Justice (Book #15)

Shameful Justice (Book #16)

Immoral Justice (Book #17)

Toxic Justice (Book #18)

Overdue Justice (Book #19)

Unfair Justice (a 10,000 word short story)

Irrational Justice (a 10,000 word short story)

Seeking Justice (a 15,000 word novella)

Caring For Justice (a 24,000 word novella)

Savage Justice (a 17,000 word novella Featuring THE UNICORN)

Clever Deception (co-written by Linda S Prather)

Tragic Deception (co-written by Linda S Prather)

Sinful Deception (co-written by Linda S Prather)

Forever Watching You (DI Miranda Carr thriller)

Wrong Place (DI Sally Parker thriller #1)

No Hiding Place (DI Sally Parker thriller #2)

Cold Case (DI Sally Parker thriller#3)

Deadly Encounter (DI Sally Parker thriller #4)

Lost Innocence (DI Sally Parker thriller #5)

Goodbye, My Precious Child (DI Sally Parker #6)

Web of Deceit (DI Sally Parker Novella with Tara Lyons)

The Missing Children (DI Kayli Bright #1)

Killer On The Run (DI Kayli Bright #2)

Hidden Agenda (DI Kayli Bright #3)

Murderous Betrayal (Kayli Bright #4)

Dying Breath (Kayli Bright #5)

Taken (Kayli Bright #6 coming March 2020)

The Hostage Takers (DI Kayli Bright Novella)

No Right to Kill (DI Sara Ramsey #1)

Killer Blow (DI Sara Ramsey #2)

The Dead Can't Speak (DI Sara Ramsey #3)

Deluded (DI Sara Ramsey #4)

The Murder Pact (DI Sara Ramsey #5)

Twisted Revenge (DI Sara Ramsey #6)

The Lies She Told (DI Sara Ramsey #7)

I Know The Truth (A psychological thriller coming June 2020)

The Caller (co-written with Tara Lyons)

Evil In Disguise – a novel based on True events

Deadly Act (Hero series novella)

Torn Apart (Hero series #1)

End Result (Hero series #2)

In Plain Sight (Hero Series #3)

Double Jeopardy (Hero Series #4)

Criminal Actions (Hero Series #5)

Regrets Mean Nothing (Hero #6)

Sole Intention (Intention series #1)

Grave Intention (Intention series #2)

Devious Intention (Intention #3)

Merry Widow (A Lorne Simpkins short story)

It's A Dog's Life (A Lorne Simpkins short story)

A Time To Heal (A Sweet Romance)

A Time For Change (A Sweet Romance)

High Spirits

The Temptation series (Romantic Suspense/New Adult Novellas)

Past Temptation

Lost Temptation

Cozy Mystery Series

Murder at the Wedding

Murder at the Hotel

Murder by the Sea

Tempting Christa (A billionaire romantic suspense co-authored by Tracie Delaney #1)

Avenging Christa (A billionaire romantic suspense co-authored by Tracie Delaney #2)

ACKNOWLEDGMENTS

Thank you as always to my rock, Jean, I'd be lost without you in my life.

Special thanks as always go to @studioenp for their superb cover design expertise.

My heartfelt thanks go to my wonderful editor Emmy Ellis, my proofreaders Joseph, Barbara and Jacqueline for spotting all the lingering nits.

Thank you also to my amazing ARC group who help to keep me sane during this process.

This one is for you, Lin, for allowing me to use your name.

To Mary, gone, but never forgotten. I hope you found the peace you were searching for my dear friend.

PROLOGUE

Laura smiled and fluttered her eyelashes at her boss. They had a flirty kind of relationship which only they understood. Laura liked Neil. Yes, he was married, but they were consenting adults, and their flirting helped to fill their day.

He had pleaded with her to stay late that evening; he was the chancellor of the university, and she was his super-efficient PA, and yes, he often took advantage of her good nature. Pleading with her to work later when he had an urgent meeting with his staff coming up. Laura was only too happy to oblige, especially when her recompense was in extra time off, which amounted to around a week's extra paid holiday. It wasn't as if she had anyone waiting for her at home anyway. She was dating Andy, but it was a casual affair so far, they'd only been together a few months. In truth, she didn't know how she felt about him. When he walked into the room, she couldn't say her heart beat rhythmically, not like it had with her previous boyfriends. He was a nice enough chap, so she put her strange feelings down to what was going on inside her, nothing that he'd done personally. Only time would tell if it would lead anywhere.

She'd promised herself to give the relationship at least another month or so before calling a halt to things. In the meantime, she'd get her kicks from other means, such as the flirting she conducted with Neil. They weren't harming anyone, were they? It all took place behind closed doors, so why shouldn't they have some fun? It definitely made the day go quicker.

"That's all the notes for now. I think we've worked hard enough today, Laura, don't you agree?" her boss said, baring his pearly whites at her, for the umpteenth time that day.

"If you think so, sir."

"Right. I'll finish off in here and walk you to the car in what, ten minutes or so?"

"I should be done by then, thank you." Laura smiled and left the office. She typed up the notes she'd scribbled and switched off her computer as Neil came out of his office and flicked the light off behind him.

"Are you ready?"

"I am." She unhooked her handbag off the back of her chair.

They chatted on the way out of the building. He told her how much he was looking forward to seeing his wife that evening, sad that he'd been forced to stay behind to work on their anniversary.

"Oh no. This could have waited, you should've said. How many years?"

"Nine, today. Honestly, I never thought we'd make it past the first couple. We totally bamboozled our friends and family, I can tell you. They all thought the same as me."

"May I ask why? Are you that different? Or is it a case of you being too similar?"

"Hard to put my finger on it, really. I'm crazy about Helen, although it doesn't stop me flirting with other women, such as yourself. You do know it's what I would term *innocent flirting*, don't you?"

"Of course. I never think anything of it. I feel the same way, it's all harmless fun, right?"

They reached her car.

Neil opened the door for her and pecked her on the cheek. "Thanks for staying behind. I think we achieved a lot tonight, much more than we had during the day with all the interruptions I've had to contend with, what with one thing or another."

"You're welcome. I love my job, it's never a chore staying behind, honestly. I'll see you in the morning. Happy anniversary to you and Helen. Enjoy the rest of your evening."

"We will. She's cooking us a special dinner. I'd better get on the road before she gets annoyed and chucks it in the bin."

Laura chuckled. "She wouldn't dare, would she?"

He raised an eyebrow. "You obviously don't know my wife."

Laura was still chortling to herself a few minutes later as she drove down Aylestone Hill in Hereford. She switched on her radio and tapped her hands on the steering wheel to a mellow tune from George Michael. That was, until the car started playing up. It jolted her forwards and then backwards in her seat, eventually grinding to a halt halfway down the hill close to the entrance of the park. She turned the key several times. The engine proved to be obstinate, refusing to spark into life and, to add to her woes, it had now started raining.

She dug in her handbag for her phone and pushed the button associated with Andy's number. It rang and rang until he finally answered, his words coming out in a slur. It was then she remembered he was on a night out with the lads. She knew it would be a waste of time asking him for help, so she hung up.

If he was that concerned about her, he'd ring back, which she seriously doubted he would.

Damn, who else can I call for help?

The truth was, she couldn't think of anyone. Her parents were away for a few days visiting her elderly grandmother in the care home after she'd taken a tumble and ended up in hospital in Manchester. Realising there was nothing else she could do, she secured the car and decided to walk the rest of the way home. *Great, and I don't even own a brolly. I'm going to get drenched. This rain is unrelenting and bouncing off the flipping pavement. I suppose I could stay with the car, but there's no telling how long I'd have to wait for someone to come to my rescue. Why didn't I renew that damn breakdown cover policy last month? I'm bloody starving, in dire need of my dinner.*

So, off she set. In her high heels, her ankles turned now and again due to the dips in the pavement, hardly the best footwear for a mile or so hike. *Oh well, them's the breaks.*

She hadn't got far when a car pulled up alongside her. At first, she ignored it, thinking it was probably a group of youths trying to wind her up. She jolted when the driver blasted his horn. He was sitting in the dark interior. He leaned over and opened the window.

"Hey, are you all right?" his cheery voice boomed out.

She peered in, trying to make out his features, but it was an impossible task. "No, my bloody car broke down about thirty yards up the road."

"Bad luck. Do you want me to have a look at it for you?"

"No, don't worry. I'll call the garage in the morning to sort it out. Thanks for stopping, though."

"I can do better than that. Do you have far to walk?"

She wiped away the raindrops splattering her face. "About a mile. I live up near the Beefeater pub, do you know it?"

"I do, I go there all the time with my missus. Hey, hop in, I'll give you a lift."

"I wouldn't want to impose on you."

"You won't be. Come on, it's on my way, no problem."

Her hair was lank and sodden, and her clothes weren't fairing much better. She decided to throw caution to the wind and take up the man's generous offer. She reached for the handle, and the door popped open. "This is so kind of you, I can't thank you enough."

"No bother. The wife would be as pleased as Punch I offered to help out; she's got a kind heart. It must be rubbing off on me after all these years."

"Aww...how long have you been married?"

He drew away from the kerb, and they continued their conversation.

"Coming up to fifteen years. I know, I don't look old enough. We were childhood sweethearts," he said, glancing sideways in her direction.

She smiled and nodded. "Your first love. That's wonderful.

Marriages don't tend to last too long nowadays, so you're both to be admired."

"We haven't had an easy ride but we make each other feel special when the need arises. It's important to keep up the date nights, right? A little romance now and again is just the ticket to stay in the wife's good books. That's my theory anyway."

Laura nodded. "That's a smart way of looking at things." She returned her gaze to the road again and frowned. "Oh my, you must've been distracted, you've taken the wrong route."

"Damn. My concentration is abysmal at times. I'll turn around up here. Can't stop yet as I have a car up my backside."

"Good idea. I suppose you can take the road to Bromyard, turn around there. My fault for engaging you in stimulating conversation, I know." She tried to laugh off the incident.

The man sniggered. "Yes, you're guilty of that all right."

The turning was lit by a streetlamp. The driver took it, however, instead of using it to turn the car around he proceeded to drive down the road.

Laura's heart pounded a little more than usual. "Umm…did you forget to turn around?"

She stared at the man.

He swivelled his head to look at her for a split second and sneered. "No. It was part of the plan."

"Umm…what does that mean?" Her voice faltered. Any thoughts of her feeling hungry were instantly crushed as her stomach clenched into a tight knot.

"Your car didn't break down all by itself, I gave it a helping hand."

"What? Who are you? Please, I don't want any trouble. Why are you doing this?"

"Questions, questions. Shut the fuck up and enjoy the ride, bitch." He put his foot down on the accelerator, and the car surged forward.

She reached for the handle but thought better of it. If she jumped out now, at this speed, well, there was no telling what would happen to her once she hit the ground. She couldn't risk it, not out here. It might have been a different story if they'd been closer to town.

Bloody hell, what do I do now? Shit! How am I going to get out of this?

Her desperate thoughts were interrupted by his snarling tone. "Sit there, be quiet, and you won't get hurt."

"Okay. Please, won't you tell me what this is all about?" The saliva filling her mouth dried up.

"What did I tell you?" His fist slammed into her nose.

The sound of breaking bones petrified her and the searing pain forced the bile up from her stomach to settle in her throat. She covered her face, the blood seeping through the gaps in her fingers. *Shit! What the hell is going on? Why did he do that? If I cry out, he'll probably hit me again.*

The man drove for another ten minutes or so. Eventually the car slowed and turned into a narrow lane which was half-gravelled with a strip of grass running down the middle. Should she try to escape now that the car had reduced speed? What if she messed up and he came after her, what would happen then? He'd already showed he wasn't concerned about hurting her.

Jesus! How the hell have I got myself into such a mess?

The car drew to an abrupt halt outside a derelict farmhouse. There was a huge Dutch barn over to the right. The man exited the car, raced around the front and wrenched her door open.

He yanked on her arm. "Get out."

With one hand still dealing with her broken nose, she left the vehicle and stared up at him. He was a good seven to eight inches taller than her, even in her high heels. "Where are we?"

"Cut out the stupid questions. You're where you need to be, that's all that matters. Move it." He shoved her in front of him, towards the barn.

Her fear notched up another level with each tentative step she took. Who was he? What did he want from her? As far as she knew, she'd never purposely upset anyone in the past, not enough to warrant them treating her like this. *Oh God, what if he's brought me here to rape me? I couldn't bear that. I'll fight for my life if he touches me down below, I just know I will.*

He unlocked the barn doors and propelled her inside. The first thing that struck her was how dark and cold the interior was. After steadying herself, she glanced up at the roof. There were dozens of gaps, letting in the elements. She shuddered, the sound of the whistling wind freaking her out even more. She had never liked being alone, let alone in a dark place like this. It made her wonder if her heart would stand up to the trauma she anticipated lay ahead of her.

Shit! Please don't leave me here, I know I won't be able to bear it.

He continued to push her farther into the barn. In the far corner were two bales of hay and a chain.

She faced him, terrified, and shook her head. "No, please, don't do this. What do you want from me? I'll do anything you want, just please, let me go."

Ignoring her, he tugged her over to the hay and threw her down, wrenching her arm in the process. The pain ripped through her, and she yelled out. It made no odds; he disregarded her complaint. Now she had a broken nose and a dislocated shoulder—at least that was what it felt like, although she was no medical expert. *Why? Who is he, and why's he treating me like this?* It was the not knowing that was eating away at her.

He wrapped the chain around her middle a few times and padlocked it to a metal loop in the wall. She presumed it was where a horse would have been tethered in days gone by. Now *she* was, but for how long? She had one thing going in her favour: he had left her hands and feet untied, for now. Should she count that as a blessing?

Once he'd secured her, he walked away.

She stretched out a pleading hand. "No, please, don't go. Why are you doing this? What have I ever done to deserve this?"

He reached the door and turned slowly to face her, a sneer pulling at his dark features. Then he tilted his head back and laughed.

1

Sara Ramsey was feeling a little more chilled out than usual. In the past week, they had solved one of the most heinous crimes she'd ever had the pleasure, or misfortune, should that be, of solving. Since then, she and the team had been tied to their desks doing the necessary paperwork to wrap up the last couple of cases. It was good having a reprieve, and she silently thanked the criminals of Hereford for behaving themselves and giving them all a much-needed break.

Life had been led at full pelt for months, significantly impacting on her personal life. Despite that, she was thrilled that Mark had recently popped the question and she couldn't help wondering if she was letting him down in some way for not giving their forthcoming wedding the attention it deserved. She'd told him, no matter what happened today, once they both got home at around six, they'd settle down after their evening meal to discuss the finer points of the wedding. That was the plan anyway. Whether it turned out that way remained to be seen.

Carla appeared in the doorway. "Can you spare me two minutes?"

Sara frowned and motioned for her partner to sit down. "Anything wrong?"

"Not really. It's personal. I need some guidance more than anything."

"I'm all ears. If I can help, you know I will. Shoot!"

Carla's gaze dropped, and she stared down at her clutched hands in her lap. Dread filled Sara at what her colleague was about to say next.

"It's the wedding…"

"Ah right! What about it?" Sara picked up a pen and laced it through her fingers to keep her hands busy.

"I'm having second thoughts."

"No. About marrying Gary? Or about the way the wedding is going?"

"Oh, God no, I still want to marry him. The thing is, his mother has taken over and is demanding that we do things her way."

"Is she really *demanding*, or is that just your perception?"

Carla tutted. "Why is it you always manage to see through me? All right, maybe she hasn't quite gone that far yet. How do I put it? She's had a massive say in the venue and where the service is going to be held."

"Okay, look at things from her point of view. I don't know the woman at all, remember. Well, what if she's doing it to help you guys? She's aware of the hours you work, and Gary's still going through his rehabilitation after his accident. Maybe she sees it as lending a hand and not necessarily as interfering."

Carla's gaze latched on to hers again. "You think?"

"From an outsider's view, yes, although I'm not seeing it from where you're sitting, of course. My advice would be to get together and discuss things with her. Maybe give her a few jobs to take care of but insist any major decisions, as you've described, should be up to you and Gary to decide on. How's that?"

"You're amazing. Crikey, if it were up to me, we'd elope. Always fancied getting married in Ireland for some reason."

"Then do it. Would Gary be up for that?"

"We've spoken about it. He loved *Game of Thrones* and has always wanted to visit that area, however…"

"The last thing he wants to do is upset his mother, right?"

"You've got it. And they wonder why weddings are deemed one of the most stressful 'chores' we have to deal with during our lives."

Sara laughed. "I think *chore* is a good word, even if it might upset a lot of people in the business. I get what you're saying. Mark and I have plans to sit down tonight and sort out our wedding details. Mind you, if my mum offered to step in and lighten the load for me, I'd snap her hand off. No chance of her doing that while she's caring for Dad, though. Makes you wonder why people like us leave it so long to get married. Doh, what am I saying? See, even I'm confused. How could I forget I've been down this route before?" She fell silent and reflected on the wonderful years she'd spent with Phillip before he had been snatched away from her. He'd been shot and murdered by a gang in Liverpool. That all seemed a lifetime away now, even though it had happened less than three years ago. She'd loved him with all her heart and could never have foreseen ever being happy again with another man, but then Mark had walked into her life. He was a vet and had saved her cat's life after someone connected to her husband's murder had poisoned it.

She'd fallen heavily, and quickly, for the man with a caring touch and an equally tender heart. It was inevitable that they would get married.

Carla cleared her throat. "Are you all right? Sorry if my complaining has stirred up old memories for you."

"Don't be daft. I'm fine. I get days when I think of Phillip. I'm bound to, he was an important part of my life."

"Do you and Mark ever discuss him? Umm…sorry, that's too personal, I shouldn't have asked."

"It's not, you're fine. I try not to speak about him. Sometimes Mark will ask out of the blue what Phillip would have done in a certain situation."

"Really? Is he that unsure of himself?"

"I wouldn't say that. He cares. Wants to do everything right to keep our relationship on track."

Carla smiled. "You were lucky to have found him."

"There's no denying that. And you're the same with Gary. Look at what you've been through the last month or so. Blimey, if you can come through that together then the future has to be rosy for you both, right?"

"I suppose so. Never really thought about it like that."

A knock on the door sounded, putting an end to their heart to heart.

"Come in," Sara shouted.

The door pushed open to reveal DCI Carol Price. "Not interrupting anything, am I?"

"No, not at all. We're going over the past few cases," Sara said, telling a white lie.

Carla rose from her seat. "I'll get back to it then."

DCI Price placed a hand on her shoulder, preventing her from rising fully. "There's no need for you to go, Carla. In fact, I think you should stay and hear this."

"I'll get another chair then." Carla left the office and returned moments later with one of the plastic chairs from the incident room and closed the door behind her. She positioned it alongside hers. The chief nodded her appreciation, and they both sat.

Carla and Sara exchanged concerned glances.

"Something wrong, boss?" Sara frowned and asked.

"Yes and no. I know you're tidying up a few cases at the moment and aren't working a live case, well…I was wondering if you'd look into something for me as a favour."

Sara tilted her head. "I'm intrigued to hear what you have to say."

Carol swallowed and then sighed. "I was contacted last night by a very dear friend of mine, a Lin Robertson. She rang me in tears, told me her daughter went missing the night before last, on Tuesday, which is totally unlike her."

"Was she reported as a missing person?"

"Yes, Laura's car was found abandoned on Aylestone Hill by her boyfriend."

"Abandoned?"

"Yes, again, it's not something she would ever likely do, according to her mother."

"I see, and where do we come into this equation?"

"I wondered if you'd have a nose around for me. Do some digging?" Carol Price grinned hopefully.

"You think there's something suspicious afoot here?" Sara asked.

"Don't you? Given what I've told you?"

Sara's gaze met Carla's, and her partner shrugged. "We could take a look. It's not as if we're dealing with anything else at present."

Sara nodded. "Okay, I'm up for it if you are. Do you know this Laura, boss?"

"Kind of. She's always tended to steer clear of me when I paid her mum a visit."

"Intentionally?"

"I wouldn't like to say. Maybe it was a teen thing. Her mother and I have sort of drifted apart the last fifteen years or so. Only dropping a card in the post to each other at Christmas or on each other's birthday. That's why I was shocked to receive the call."

"I see. All right, as we're free at the moment then it'll be our pleasure to take the case on. Will you pave the way for us with the super?"

"I will. He'll probably give you the green light with the instructions to leave the case once something meatier comes along. I'll be fine with that." She took a sheet of paper from her jacket pocket and handed it to Sara across the desk. "That's Lin's address and phone number. I took a punt you'd accept the investigation and told her to expect a call from you."

"You know me so well." Sara chortled. "Anything else you think we should know?"

"Not really. Her mum will be able to fill you in more about her character in recent years and any other general information." Carol left her seat and made her way to the door. "Do your best. If something bad has happened, then we could be against the clock on this one."

"Don't worry, we'll bear that in mind. I'll ring Lin now and make arrangements to go and see her."

"Thanks. Keep me up to date."

"I will."

Once the door was closed, Sara let out a large breath. "Damn, that's all we need. I've dealt with cases personal to a superior before and I can tell you, they never turn out satisfactorily."

"A lot of added pressure, you mean?"

"Yep. My betting is the chief will be in here morning and evening, demanding to know what the developments are, if any."

"Could you blame her for that?"

"No, I suppose not. Get me a coffee, would you? I'll ring Lin once the caffeine hits my system."

Carla leapt out of her seat. She returned carrying a steaming coffee and set it on Sara's desk. "I'll get on with tying up a few loose ends until you give me the nod."

"Thanks, Carla. I shouldn't be too long, I hope."

She took several sips of coffee and then plucked up the courage to pick up her phone and ring the DCI's friend. "Hello, Mrs Robertson. I'm DI Sara Ramsey. I believe you're expecting my call."

"Oh my. Thank you so much for ringing, Carol told me you're her best officer. Oops, maybe I betrayed her confidence there, ignore me."

Sara laughed. "That's high praise indeed. We'll keep that a secret between us. Would it be possible for me and my partner to pop round to see you?"

"Oh yes, that would be so much better. I'm not the most confident person on the phone. When can you come?"

"You're in Whitestone, yes?"

"That's right."

"We should be with you within the next twenty minutes, once I've instructed the team what to do in my absence."

"I'll make sure the kettle is boiled for when you get here."

"Lovely, I never say no to a nice cup of coffee. We'll see you soon."

"Goodbye."

Sara stared down at her half-filled cup and decided to leave the rest of it, what with the promise of another fresh cup awaiting her at the other end. She tidied away the few papers she was dealing with and rejoined the team in the incident room.

"No doubt Carla has brought you up to speed on what the DCI has

THE LIES SHE TOLD

just handed us. What I need is for you all to finish doing what you can on the other cases, clear the desks for us to give our all for this one, especially as it involves one of the chief's friends. Carla, are you ready to go?"

Her partner swigged the remains of her coffee and nodded. "I am now."

Together they left the building. The Hereford weather was touch and go that morning. One minute they were driving through a shower and the next Sara was reaching for her sunglasses, blinded by the rays. "Anyone would think it was April instead of February. There's talk of a bad storm coming in over the weekend."

"Not looking forward to that. Look at the flooding we've been dealing with since October." Carla pointed at the fields on either side of the A4103 which had been under at least two or three feet of water since the autumn.

She nodded, imagining the devastation more rain could do if it fell like the weathermen predicted. Numerous rivers were already near their limits in the area as it was. Sara followed the satnav's direction and drew up outside an older-style property with a gated entrance. Sara left the car outside the gates and found the side one open to visitors.

"Nice house," Carla noted.

"Looking a little tired around the edges, but yes, I agree. Nice area, too, compared to some parts of Hereford."

"Yeah, the council are doing their best to improve things. We had a bad reputation for being the drug capital in these parts around twenty years ago."

"I wasn't aware of that fact. I've not seen much evidence of that since I've arrived, not in comparison to what I experienced in Liverpool."

"I think all the druggies moved to Worcester."

"Good for us, bad for the police over there. Let's see what she has to say."

Lin Robertson opened the door before Sara had a chance to knock. Her eyes had black rings around them, implying she hadn't slept much the previous night. She tried to smile, but it didn't last long. "Hello, I'm Lin. You must be the inspector I spoke to on the phone earlier."

"Yes, DI Sara Ramsey, and this is my partner, DS Carla Jameson."

She held the door open wider, stepped back and gestured for them to enter. "Come through to the lounge. My husband is waiting in there."

Her husband was a man who looked as if he had the weight of the world on his shoulders. He was standing by the oak mantel above the open fire, smoking a cigarette.

"Hello, sir," Sara said, smiling at the gentleman.

"Hello, come in. Sorry if I'm a little abrupt, but I'm eager to get on with things. That girl has been missing since Tuesday, and we're desperate to know where she is."

"That girl? You mean your daughter, right?" Sara queried.

"No, she's my stepdaughter—that doesn't mean I don't think the world of her, I do. We brought her up together from the age of five, so yes, I think of her as my own flesh and blood."

"I see. Thank you for clarifying that so succinctly. And her real father? Is he still alive?"

The couple glanced at each other and rolled their eyes.

"He's a waste of space. He's flitted in and out of her life over the years, absent for most of it, until the guilt seeps in, and then he shows up like a goddamn bad smell," Lin said, her tone filled with bitterness, and possibly anger.

"That's right. He hasn't been around for years. At least ten to my knowledge," Mr Robertson added.

"Thank you. Do you know where he's living now?"

"Ha, that man moves around and lives like a bloody nomad. He usually shows up when he's short of cash. At least that's what he's done in the past," Mr Robertson informed them.

Sara smiled. "His last known address would help us."

"I think I have it in an old address book. You don't think he's responsible for Laura going missing, do you?" Lin replied, crossing the room to a set of drawers made from walnut along the far wall. She opened the top one and roughly moved the contents around until she found what she was looking for and returned to the group. "Here it is."

"It's too soon to say. Carla, can you take down his details for me?" Sara asked.

Her partner scribbled down the information and handed the book back to Lin who took a seat on the grey fabric sofa and laid the book in her lap. Mr Robertson moved to sit next to her, and they held hands as Carla and Sara also took their seats.

"What can you tell me about your daughter's disappearance?" Although DCI Price had gone through what they suspected had happened, it was always good for a detective to hear the news firsthand from the relatives.

"She was working late at the college, according to her boyfriend, Andy. She often works late for her boss. Andy rung us around midnight to see if she had stayed over with us. He'd got home from a night out with the lads and found the house empty."

"As you can imagine, we've been frantic ever since. As soon as it was light, Jack and I went out looking for her. Andy volunteered to join us. He was the one who found Laura's car, close to the park."

"She wouldn't have left it there like that, not without ringing one of us. Andy said she rang his number but he was drunk and didn't realise it was her until it was too late," Mr Robertson added.

"Any reason why she didn't think to ring you?"

Lin sighed. "We've been away caring for Jack's mother; she had a fall and spent some time in hospital. When the hospital released her, Jack's sister assured us she could manage, so we came back early. Laura thought we were coming home tomorrow, therefore, I don't think she would have thought about ringing us if she was in trouble, not if she thought we were up north still."

Sara smiled. "I see. Try not to blame yourself."

Lin nodded. "It's that obvious, eh?"

"It is. It's really not going to solve anything in the long run. We'll find her, it's only a matter of time. What can you tell me about her boyfriend? Andy, is it?"

"Yes, Andy Palmer…" Her gaze dropped to the carpet.

Sara's gut instinctively clenched. "Lin, if there's something you think we should know, it would be better to tell us up front."

Lin sucked in a large breath and nodded. "He's an ex-con. And yes, we've had the conversation with her about not trusting him, the one about leopards and spots et cetera, but you know how stubborn people can be once they've lost their heart to someone."

"She loves him then? Have they been together very long?"

"Around six months, I believe, isn't it, Jack?"

Jack nodded, sat back in his chair and folded his arms. "We did try to dissuade her from moving in with him, but it fell on deaf ears, and she's thirty-six, for fuck's sake. Pardon me, excuse my language."

"I take it you don't get on with Andy, sir?"

"In small doses. He's one of those cocksure types that piss me off."

His wife tutted at his use of bad language again. "You'll have to excuse my husband, he doesn't usually swear in front of ladies. It's the stress, Inspector."

Sara waved the apology away. "Don't worry, we hear far worse down the station during lunchtime, I can assure you. Maybe I shouldn't have revealed that," she replied light-heartedly, in an attempt to ease the sudden tension in the room. It did the trick as Mr and Mrs Robertson smiled briefly. "We'll need his address, too, if you don't mind?"

Lin flipped open the address book again, and Carla shot out of her seat, jotted down the information and then returned to sit alongside Sara once more.

"Laura moved in with him around three months ago. Up until then she was living with us."

"Out of necessity or choice?"

"Necessity. Her first marriage broke up three years ago. She's been saving up, trying to get back on her feet, to be able to afford another house. You know what a task that is for young people these days."

"That's true. Did she move in with Andy then, or did they buy a place together?"

"She moved into his place. His gran left him a property when she died around four or five months ago, I believe. Don't quote me on that, though."

"Duly noted. Thank you. I have to ask what their relationship is like. Before you answer that, I'm aware of how people hide the truth from their parents. What I suppose I'm asking is whether you've had any cause for concern lately."

"No, not that I can think of, except for the money aspect," Lin said.

"In what way?"

"She always seems to be broke, not that she ever asks us for any help financially. We just assumed that she was finding it hard to adjust."

"Okay, that gives us a little to go on. We can take a look at her bank account, see what's going on there."

"You can? That would be great. I'm sure she keeps a lot from us. It would be interesting to know if the money she'd saved up over the past few years is still sitting in her account."

"Do you know how much that's likely to be?"

"Around twenty-three thousand, I believe. We took very little from her in the way of rent."

Jack growled in annoyance. "Yes, that was always a sore point between my wife and me. That's by the by, though. We just want to know where Laura is and if she's safe. The money no longer matters, not to me."

If that's the case, why bring it up?

"Hopefully, we'll get to the bottom of it soon. What about the ex-husband, any issues there you think we should be aware of?"

Lin raised her eyebrows. "Are you saying you think he might have something to do with this?"

"We need to dig into every aspect of your daughter's life. It seems obvious to start with those she's fallen out with in the past. I'm taking it they didn't part amicably? People rarely do these days."

"That's true. He went off with a young bit of skirt, not sure what she does for a living," Lin said. She turned to face her husband when he knocked his leg against hers.

"Yes, you do. She's a hairdresser or something along those lines in Hereford town centre, I'm sure she is."

Lin nodded and faced Sara again. "Silly me. Now Jack has mentioned it, she's a beautician in one of the salons in town, don't ask me which one."

"I won't. Do you have an idea of their home address perhaps? I know it's asking a lot."

"Not at all. Sorry, I don't have it. His name is Bobby Tyler. They sold the house they were living in and split the proceeds, not that there was that much to divvy out as the house was mortgaged to the hilt. Another bloke not good with money."

"Oi, you. I've always been good with it. Don't go tarring me with the same brush, lady." Jack's response was issued jokingly.

Sara suspected they'd held the same conversation numerous times in the past.

"What about other boyfriends or man friends she's had? Anyone dubious in her history?"

Lin shook her head. "No, I don't think so. She was married to Bobby for around ten years. I can't for the life of me think of any of the fellas she went out with before he came along. That might be because my mind is all over the place and I'm not thinking straight right now."

"You can get back to me on that, I'll leave you my card. I appreciate how stressful all this is for you."

"It's the not knowing." Lin buried her face in her hands and broke down.

Her husband sat forward and slung a clumsy arm around her shoulders. "Now, Lin, what did I tell you about getting yourself upset like this? It's not going to do you any good. That girl will be expecting you to remain positive at all times."

She dropped her hands and wiped her tears and nose on a tissue she took from her sleeve and sniffed. "I know. I can't help it, my mind is going through all different scenarios. I need you to take this seriously. My daughter wouldn't have just disappeared like this, not without a reason. And all I can think is that someone has taken her."

It was obvious how distraught the poor woman was.

"I'm sorry you think that. We're going to do our best to find her. It's not usually our field of expertise, we have a specified missing persons team, however, we're doing this as a favour to our boss. I want to assure you, we will go above and beyond what's expected of us."

Lin offered a grateful smile. "Thank you, that truly means a lot. I hope it indicates that you'll find her soon."

"I have to ask… Do you think there's a possibility she might have run off? Left everything and just done a bunk?"

"Is she likely to do that? Wouldn't she need her vehicle if that was her intention?" Jack asked, his brow furrowed by the suggestion.

"Okay, there is that. It was just a thought." Sara's mind was working overtime now, however, she reined in the rest of her thoughts and decided she would share them with her partner once they left the house. "What about her job, was that going well?"

"Yes, she works at the higher education college at the top of Aylestone Hill on the roundabout. She hasn't complained so I presume she must like it there."

"How long has she worked there? Is she a teacher?"

"No, she's a PA to the chancellor of the college. She's been there around three years, since her marriage ended. She loves working there, said her boss is very fair."

"That's good to know. We'll drop by and have a chat with him all the same, especially as she was working late at the college before she went missing."

"I can understand that. It's why her car was left on the side of the road that gets to me. Surely if she had trouble starting it, wouldn't she have left it at the college and either got a lift from her boss or called a taxi?"

"Possibly. We'll see what forensics have to say about the vehicle. We should know that within a few days or so."

"Fingers crossed. Is there anything else you need to know, Inspector?" Lin asked.

"I don't think so. We'll crack on. The sooner we start questioning people, the better. I'll be in touch shortly, I hope. Ring me if you think of anything else we should know." She rose from her seat, followed by Carla, and handed Lin a business card.

Lin gave it to her husband and showed them to the front door.

"Please, do your best. I appreciate it's not your usual line of work."

Sara touched Lin's arm. "Don't worry. We'll work just as hard on this case as we do with every other case that drops onto my desk. Take care of yourself and try not to worry in the meantime. I know that's going to be hard, but if you work yourself up into a state then you're not going to be doing either yourself or your family any favours."

"I'll try my best. Good luck."

Sara smiled and stepped out of the house. She and Carla headed back to the car.

"What do you think?" Carla asked as they prepared to get into the vehicle.

"I was just about to ask you the same." Sara smiled across the roof of the car. She looked back at the house and saw the couple standing at the lounge window, waving them off. Her heart went out to them, and she waved back. Inside the car, Sara sighed. "It's a toughie. Like her mother said, if there was something wrong with her car, why didn't she leave it where it was and grab a taxi? We should track her phone, see what we get from that."

"That was my first thought as well. Do you want me to ask one of the team to action that?"

"Yeah, if you would. I'm going to drive over to the home she shared with this boyfriend. I'm dying to see what type of character he is."

Sara started the car and listened to Carla instruct Jill Smalling back at the station as to what they needed. Carla gave their colleague Laura Tyler's address and phone number which Lin had supplied and asked Jill to do the necessary checks. She also asked her to give the details of Bobby Tyler to another member of the team to try to locate him. Finally, Carla instructed Jill to see what the team could find out about Laura's real father, Phil Jackson, address unknown at this point.

Carla ended the call. "They're on it and will get back to us ASAP with the details."

"Good. Let's hope the information is easy to track down. According to the satnav, we're almost there. I can't say I'm looking forward to this encounter, especially if he's an ex-con. You know how they react to being questioned."

"I do. Maybe I should have got one of them to check out his record. The mother didn't say what he'd been inside for, did she?"

"I don't think she did. I should have asked. A rap on the knuckles for me there. I suppose in my defence, I saw how upset she was and kept any probing questions to a minimum in the hope she wouldn't dwell on them once we'd gone."

"I get that. It doesn't help us, though."

"I know. Perhaps Andy will be the obliging sort." Carla leaned forward and made a show of searching the sky. Sara slapped her leg and said, "I know what you're doing, looking out for that elusive flying snouted creature."

Carla sniggered. "Yep, I thought I'd better check."

"Here we are. This place seems okay, not as nice as where her parents live, but I wouldn't describe it as a dive either. Have you been to the Beefeater for a meal?"

"You're always thinking of your stomach," Carla noted, shaking her head.

"No, I'm not, and you didn't answer my question. I went the other week with Mark, and it was a delicious meal."

"I went years ago. Rarely come over this side of town if I'm honest. I'll give it a try soon. I might even treat Gary, although he'll probably pounce on me and tell me not to waste our money with the wedding coming up."

"You should be grateful he's good with money. A lot of men don't know what it's like to save for something, as Lin just mentioned. I'm inclined to agree with her, too."

"You're referring to the problems your sister has had with her recent fella, aren't you?"

"Yeah, amongst others. Let's not go down that route. She's well shot of that fucker, I can tell you."

2

Sara parked the car on the street and approached the small terraced house. There was no flaking paint, and the garden appeared to be in pristine condition, which surprised Sara for some reason she found hard to pinpoint. Maybe she was guilty of judging Andy before she laid eyes on him. She reprimanded herself and rang the bell.

The door opened after a few minutes to reveal a blond man with messed-up hair. He was dressed in ripped jeans and a baggy black T-shirt which had seen better days.

Offering up her ID for him to look at, Sara announced, "DI Sara Ramsey, and this is my partner, Carla Jameson. Would you be Andy?"

"I am. This is about Laura, right? Stupid question, you don't have to answer that. Come in if you like."

"It is, and thanks. We'd like to ask you a few questions."

"I've been expecting you." He slammed the door shut once Sara and Carla entered the hallway. "Go through to the back of the house. I'm eating my breakfast—you don't mind, do you?"

"No, go ahead." Sara led the way. The kitchen was large enough to fit a small round table and four chairs. The units were old-fashioned and pine. She heaved at the smell of burning fat.

"Yeah, sorry about the smell, I burnt the bacon while I nipped to the loo. Take a seat or stand if you prefer. I want to dig in, otherwise it's gonna get cold."

"You carry on. I'm going to stand, just in case I have to bolt for the loo. Sorry, I hate the smell of burning fat at the best of times."

He stood and flung the back door open. "It'll clear soon. I ain't gonna keep apologising to ya."

"I wasn't expecting you to." *Great, well, that's us off to a decent start then.*

"Good. What do you want to know?" he asked, dipping a bread soldier into a snotty fried egg that added to her stomach-churning experience.

"We've just come from Laura's parents'. Her mother mentioned that Laura tried to call you the night she went missing, is that right?"

"You know it is. Not sure what you expect me to say."

Sara groaned inwardly. It was going to be like that, was it? Well, two could play at that game. He gathered another forkful of fry-up. Sara slammed her hand onto the table, scaring the shit out of him.

He spluttered and almost choked on his snotty egg. "What the fuck is going on?"

"Cut the frigging attitude. We have every right to be here asking questions about a missing person. We can do without you being obtrusive, okay?"

"I wasn't aware I was. All I want to do is eat my breakfast before it gets cold and claggy, is there a law against that?"

Her blood heated to a high temperature. "Jesus, don't you care?"

"Fuck off. Of course I care, I wouldn't have rung her parents if I didn't."

"I notice you didn't ring the police direct. Why is that?"

He finished the mouthful he was eating before he answered, his chewing slow and deliberate, which only ticked Sara off more.

"You know why, I don't have to spell it out for you. Any good copper would've done the background searches on the family, and me, by now."

"That's the smartest thing you've said since we arrived. We know you have a record, lots of people do, but it doesn't stop them from picking up the phone when they suspect something major has happened to their other half."

He continued to eat the final mouthful and then pushed the plate away and sat back. "So, let's not beat about the bush here. You're suggesting I've done something to her, right?"

Sara looked at Carla. "Did I say that?"

Carla shrugged. "I don't think so, no."

"Ha, ha. You two make a good double act, I'd say along the lines of *Dumb and Dumber* but I'd probably get my arse kicked."

Sara blew out an exasperated breath and pointed at him. "You really are pissing me off now, buster. What exactly are you trying to prove with this shitty attitude of yours?"

"Not much. I know what you tossers are like. Someone gets put in the clink, then released, and they remain on the radar for years, even if they've turned over a new leaf."

"And have you? Turned over a new leaf?"

"Yeah. I'm on the straight now. Laura has seen to that."

"Good to hear. So, for Laura's sake, stop frigging messing with us. You want her found, don't you?"

He nodded. "That's the idea and why I rang her parents. There was no point in me ringing you. Your lot don't tend to treat my sort well."

"Wrong perception there. The bonus is that Laura's mother has a friend high up in the force; we're doing this as a favour."

He raised his eyebrows and picked at his off-white teeth. "Ah, I'm with you, it's a case of not what you know but who, right?"

"I suppose you could say that. Why don't you tell us what happened on Tuesday night?"

"In what respect?"

Sara tutted. "You're not making this bloody easy. Where were you?"

"Out on the piss, with my mates."

"That much I'm aware of. *Where*?"

"The Three Feathers. My mates will verify that—oh, and the landlord, Jeff, will as well."

Sara caught a glimpse of Carla taking out her notebook in her peripheral vision. "Names of your friends?"

He folded his arms and glared at her. "Why?"

"That's obvious, at least it should be."

"Obvious in that you think I'm lying, and you want to get to the truth, is that it?"

"No, we're going to need to check out everyone's story, not just yours."

"Ah, so, her parents, you're going to check out their alibis as well, yes?"

"Yes, of course," Sara bluffed to appease him.

"Good, well then, that makes sense. Tory, Lee and Warren were there with me."

"Do these three have surnames?"

"Probably. Don't ask me what they are. I don't know theirs and they probably don't know mine, we don't go in for all that."

"All right. What time did you get to the pub?"

"Around eight, an early start for us. Didn't take me long to get bladdered, though. I was in the mood to make the most of my freedom."

"May I ask why?"

"No reason. God, you really do want to know the ins and outs of a donkey's anus, don't you?"

Sara stared and held his gaze until he looked down. "What time did you get the call from Laura?"

"Around nine or thereabouts. Oh, I don't know."

"Where's your phone? That will tell us."

"Doh! Silly me, of course it will."

He left the room and returned carrying his mobile. He punched in the password then handed it to Sara. "There it is, nine-ten."

"And you were drunk by then?"

"Yeah, what about it? It's not a crime to have a few bevvies when the missus is working, is it?"

"No, it's not. Did you speak to her?"

"No. I answered, couldn't hear what she was saying and hung up.

Thought I'd ring her back in a few minutes, after I finished my pint but..."

"Don't tell me, it slipped your mind."

"It did. I was having too much fun to care."

Sara snorted. "Nice of you. Does she usually call you when she knows you're on a night out?"

"No."

"And that didn't spark a warning sign in that head of yours?"

"Don't bloody have a go at me. My mind was elsewhere."

"Was there another lady with you?"

"Bollocks, don't go thinking that, lady cop. I ain't like that," he snarled and flopped back into his seat.

"Simple question, there's no need for you to lose your rag with me."

"I ain't. This ain't going well because of my past record. You need to forget about that. I've been on the straight and narrow for at least a year."

"How long have you been seeing Laura?"

"I don't know, four, maybe five months."

"How do you feel about her?"

"What type of question is that?"

"I'd say it was a very important one," Sara replied, holding his gaze. There was something about this guy that made the hackles rise on the back of her neck. Something she had trouble analysing. Maybe the background search would shed more light on that once they got it underway.

"She lives with me, how do you think I *feel* about her?"

"Is it a serious relationship?" Sara probed.

"I repeat, she lives with me, so yes, I'd say it's serious."

"Okay, at least we're getting somewhere now."

He shook his head. "You're unbelievable."

"No, I'm trying to ascertain what has happened to Laura. Her parents seem distraught by her disappearance, and we come here to find you appearing to take things in your stride."

"What? How do you frigging work that one out?"

Sara's gaze landed on the plate and then worked its way back up to his face.

"Jesus, because I knocked myself up a bloody breakfast. What am I supposed to do, starve?"

"I'm not saying that. Okay, we're wasting time here."

"I should say."

"Has Laura shown any signs that there was anything wrong personally, lately?"

He frowned. "Like what?"

"Has she had a run-in with anyone? Mentioned that she thought someone was following her? That sort of thing."

"Nope, nothing. If someone had been following her, I would've knocked seven bells of shit out of them. Is that what you think, that someone has taken her?"

"Don't you?"

"I haven't got the foggiest. I keep ringing her phone, and it's dead."

"Was everything okay between you?"

"As far as I know, yeah. We don't live in each other's pockets. She goes out with her friends the same as I go out with mine, if that's your next question."

"It was. Thank you. Is there anything else you can tell us?"

"No, nothing that I can think of. Please, I know I can be a right shit at times, but there's no way I'd hurt her. I'm worried about her safety. You should be out there looking for her."

"In an ideal world we'd be doing that, however, it's vital that we speak to those around her first to obtain a picture of her character and see if there was anything amiss in her life, so bear with us. What about her friends, you've mentioned them already. Do you have their names and numbers?"

"No, she would have all that in her phone. The truth is, about her friends, they haven't come near the joint—they haven't warmed to our relationship, shall we say. That's their loss, not ours. She's been seeing them less and less lately."

"Because they don't want to know you?"

"I'm assuming. Laura was quite happy being at home with me, so it didn't bother her. She's been out with her friends once a month since we got together, her choice, not mine."

"And how often have you been out with your friends, Andy?"

"Twice a week. Also, my choice, she was all right with that as well, before you come down heavy on me."

They were getting nowhere fast. Sara didn't know enough about the victim to start digging deeper than that at present, so she decided to wrap things up. "Okay, well, thanks for seeing us."

"Is that it?"

"Unless there's anything you've got for us?"

"Not really. Wait, hang on… Try Cassandra, or Cas, Wells. She's closer to Laura than anyone else."

"Her phone number or address would be helpful."

"Sorry, no can do. I haven't got a scooby doo."

"Anyone else you can think of who we can speak to?"

"Nope. If you can get to Cas, she can give you the rest of the information you need."

"I hope so. Do you work, Andy?"

"Yep, I rang in sick today, that's how concerned I am about Laura."

"What do you do?"

"I'm a delivery driver, for my sins. The only job I could get after being inside. Not many places are keen to open their doors to an ex-con."

"I'm sure. Okay, I'll leave you a card. If you hear or think of anything else we should know, don't hesitate to contact me."

He took the card and stood. Sara and Carla followed him out into the hallway.

He opened the front door. "Please find her, I'm worried about her safety."

"We're going to do our very best. Thanks for your time." Sara allowed her partner to leave the house first and felt the draught of the door slamming behind her. "Charming individual."

They got back in the car. "Want me to dig into his past?" Carla had her mobile poised.

"Yeah, definitely. We need to find out what he was inside for. I'm in two minds about him. What did you get from our conversation?"

"I wouldn't trust him at all. What a pig, eating his breakfast as if nothing had happened. Not sure how I prevented myself from puking up. The smell was horrendous."

"Yep, I'm with you on that one, another reason why I ended the interview early. I need to find out more about him before we bring him in for further questioning. Something doesn't sit well with me. I'm not sure if my instinct is going on his past record, though. Ring the station, get them on to that now."

"I'm on it."

"I think we should visit her boss next. See what he has to say."

Carla rang the station, and Sara selected first gear and pulled away from the kerb. She shook her head, not liking the way things had gone so far, fearing that Laura was as much out of their reach as she was first thing.

3

Sara parked at the end of the car park, in the only space available to her. She waited for Carla to finish her call and to apprise her of the situation, then they left the vehicle and entered the main entrance of the glass-fronted college.

"Barry's going to dig deep into Andy's record and get back to us ASAP."

"Great, we can't do anything until we know more there. Let's ask at the reception desk."

There was a pretty young brunette sitting behind the desk. "Hello, how can I help?"

Sara flashed her ID. "We'd like to see the person in charge."

"Oh, okay, that would be Mr Armitage. I'll give him a call, see if he can squeeze you in."

"Thanks." Sara took a few paces back from the desk and surveyed her surroundings. The area was flooded with light, and there were several statues bathed in sunlight in the reception area. The statues were formed from different materials, some of which she had a problem recognising. She imagined they'd been constructed by the students at the art college.

"Mr Armitage won't be long, he's on his way down."

Sara smiled at the receptionist, turned and watched a man in his forties arrive at the top of the stairs and make his way down to them.

"Hello, you wanted to see me. I'm Neil Armitage."

Sara showed the man her ID and introduced herself and Carla. "Is there somewhere private where we can have a chat, sir?"

"Of course, my office is upstairs. Come this way."

During their journey, Sara asked, "All these statues, were they created by the students?"

"Yes, students past and present. We've been privileged to teach some impressively talented individuals over the years, as you can see."

"Some of them, well, *most* of them are truly amazing I have to say."

The conversation halted until they reached the next level and Armitage showed them into his office. Again, Sara's eye was drawn to the dominating feature which was a wall of glass overlooking the beautiful tree-filled gardens beyond.

"Quite stunning, isn't it?" He beamed, following her awestruck gaze.

"And some. I wish my office had a view like this. Mind you, I probably wouldn't get much work done."

"Please, take a seat."

The three of them sat.

Mr Armitage linked his fingers together and asked, "May I enquire what this is about, Inspector?"

"Laura Tyler."

His brow wrinkled, and he shifted in his chair. "Ah, okay. What about her?"

"I take it she hasn't shown up for work today?"

"No. I was a little concerned about that. I haven't seen her since Tuesday. I've tried to call her several times, but her mobile appears to be dead. Is she okay?"

"The honest answer would be we don't know. She appears to have gone missing."

"Oh my, I just thought she was tucked up in bed with the flu or something, never dreamed there was something wrong."

"According to her mother, she worked late with you on Tuesday night, is that correct?"

"Yes, that's right. We worked until around nine and left then. Laura is always willing to stay behind when I need her to. We have an arrangement that she has the time added to any holidays due."

"I see. How did she seem when you last saw her?"

"In good spirits. Eager to go home for something to eat, I think. Missing, you say. May I ask how you know that?"

"Her car was found abandoned close to the park down the hill by her boyfriend. She tried to ring him—he was on a night out and forgot to ring her back. Since then he's tried to call her several times and, like you, he found her phone unresponsive."

"Oh heck, where on earth could she be?"

"That's our job to find out. May I ask how close you are to her, sir?"

"I'm not sure what you mean by that."

"She's your PA, I understand. I wondered if she ever confided in you."

"Ah, I see, not as such. We have a very good working relationship, but I suppose you'd say we keep our private lives separate. Please don't make me feel guilty about that."

"That truly wasn't my aim. Can you tell me what sort of mood she was in on Tuesday?"

"Yes, she appeared to be fine. Her usual self, in fact. What are you suggesting? That she was troubled and might have done some harm to herself?"

"Possibly. At the moment, we're simply trying to ascertain what state of mind she was in, if anything was likely to be upsetting her. The truth is, we're in the dark as to what might've happened to her and we need some itsy-bitsy clue to get the investigation going."

"Okay. Then you're looking in the wrong place. Laura is the ultimate professional while at work. She leaves her personal life at the front door, we all do around here. We have a very steady ship running here."

"Glad to hear it. What about her colleagues, was she close to any of them?"

"I don't think so. Laura is devoted to her work, she spends most of her lunches at her desk, only nipping out for the odd loo break, therefore, she doesn't really mix with any of the others."

"She does sound an exceptional woman. I take it you're pleased with her work?"

"Of course. She always gives a thousand percent while she's here."

"And that hasn't faltered in the past week or so?"

"No, not in the slightest. If anything, she's worked harder than ever this week; Tuesday night was a prime example. She spent as much time on the premises as I did. We put in a thirteen-hour day. This is an exceptionally busy time of the year, what with the exams just around the corner."

"I see. So, you worked the long hours and left together, is that right?"

"Yes. I said farewell to her at the car, and we went our separate ways. I can't believe you're telling me she's missing."

"Did you see anyone hanging around the car park perhaps?"

"No. Oh God, this is inconceivable." He raked a hand through his short dark hair.

"Do you have CCTV footage?"

"Yes, yes, we do. Do you want me to call the head of security and get the disc sorted for you? I'm willing to do anything to help you out, Inspector."

"That would be very kind of you. Just the night in question will do, it'll help immensely."

He picked up the phone, punched in a number and had a brief conversation with Eric, the security guard, then he hung up and smiled. "Eric is sorting that out for you now, he shouldn't be too long. Can I get you a drink while you're waiting?" He pointed off to the left to the coffee percolator sitting on a table against the wall.

Sara declined. "We're fine, thank you. You mentioned that you never discuss personal issues. You're aware that she has a boyfriend, yes?"

"Of course, Andy, why?"

"Did she tell you about his background or hint at what kind of relationship they had?"

"I know nothing about his background. She did say she'd moved in with him a few months ago, so I presumed it must be serious between them."

"I see. Well, I can't think of any other questions to ask you right now."

"I'll show you out. We can drop in on Eric on the way downstairs."

The three of them left the office and descended the stairs.

"Wait here, I won't be long."

Sara and Carla observed some of the paintings on the nearby wall while they waited.

"Any interest in art?" Sara asked.

Carla shook her head. "Matchstick men, that's all I managed to paint at school."

"It didn't seem to do Lowry any harm." Sara chuckled.

"Who?"

She shook her head. "It doesn't matter."

Mr Armitage appeared and gave Sara the disc. "There you are. It's a copy, no need to return it to me."

"Thanks, that's very kind of you."

They left the building.

Once they were seated in the car, Sara exhaled. "Shit, what the hell is going on here? How are we supposed to pick up a lead if no one can tell us anything?"

"Why do you think that is? Are you thinking it's deliberate?"

Sara tutted. "I don't know. As I said back there, I'm not getting anything from this case so far, which in my mind doesn't bode well."

"Let's pass it over then."

"Are you kidding? I'd never be able to be in the same room as the boss again if I gave up now. What I'm saying is…I suppose this is the first time I've been out of my comfort zone."

"What do you want me to do to help?"

THE LIES SHE TOLD

"My guess is we're going to be relying on the information the team can provide for now."

"Want me to contact the station, see what they have for us?"

"Yep, do that. I need a coffee. Let's stop at the café down the road, and we can use the time to make some notes between us."

Carla rang the station and put the phone on speaker. "Hi, Jill, have you got anything for us?"

"Hi, yes, some of what you needed. We've tracked down the ex-husband, he lives at nineteen Turnpike Road in the centre of town, near enough. The father we're still trying to trace. He's proving difficult to find at present, a bit of a free spirit and prefers to up sticks frequently, according to one of his previous landlords."

"Shit! Not helpful, keep trying," Sara replied. "Anything with Laura's phone yet?"

"No, boss, it's dead. My take is it's either been dumped or the SIM card has been removed. Either way, no use to us."

"Bugger. I feel like we're going around in circles already and we've only been at this a few hours."

"We're doing our best, boss," Jill said.

"I wasn't insinuating you weren't, Jill, it's just my frustration rearing its head earlier than anticipated. We've questioned the parents, the boss and the boyfriend so far, and none of them can give us a bloody clue as to where to begin our investigation."

"Sorry to hear that. I'm sure you'll get a break soon."

"Here's hoping. We've got a few things to add to your load. As well as digging into Andy's record, Barry's already on that, I also need you to trace a Cassandra Wells. Apparently, she's Laura's best friend. The boyfriend couldn't tell us her address or phone number. I'd like that ASAP."

"On it now. I'll ring you back."

"Speak soon, Jill. Thanks."

Carla jabbed her finger at the phone to end the call.

Sara drove to a small café they had passed earlier and parked in the car park at the rear. They ordered a coffee each, and Sara persuaded

Carla to indulge in a cream cake. They deserved the treat after the morning they'd had so far.

Sara was halfway through her coffee éclair, and Carla had just opened her mouth to take a chunk off her cake, when her phone rang.

"Saved by the bell. My hips will appreciate that." Carla answered the call. "Hi, Jill. Want to speak to the boss? We've stopped off at a café, so I can't put it on speaker."

Carla handed the phone over.

Sara hurriedly wiped her hands and mouth on a serviette. "Sorry for the delay, Jill. What news do you have?"

"Hold on to your hat."

Sara sucked in a breath then let it out slowly. "Go on, I'm prepared."

"The boyfriend was in the nick for raping a girl and is on the sex offenders' register."

"Shit. I knew there was something dodgy about the little bugger. Although he had us believing he's been on the straight since coming out."

"And I have an address for Cassandra Wells for you."

"Hang on, I'll get Carla to take it down."

Carla scrabbled to get her notebook out and poised her pen.

"Okay, she's ready."

"Flat three, Waldorf Street. Again, it's close to the town centre."

Sara repeated the information, and Carla mouthed, "I know where that is, I think."

"Good, Carla said she knows it. Thanks, Jill, keep up the good work back there. We'll go and see what the friend says and probably come back to the station after."

"Good luck. Over and out."

Sara ended the call and slid the phone across the table to Carla. She lowered her voice and said, "He's a rapist and on the sex offenders' list."

"Bloody hell, I wonder if Laura knew that."

"Your guess is as good as mine. I'm going to take a punt on this and make him our main suspect."

"Really? Just because of his record?"

"His record, plus I think it's convenient that he was out the night she went missing. A perfect alibi, wouldn't you say?"

"If I had a devious mind to think that way, then yes. Why would he do it? How? You think he got someone else involved?"

"Maybe, I don't know. The truth is, we don't know enough about anything just yet. Makes sense why he was spiky with us, right?"

"Yeah. If he's innocent I can understand his attitude, something to be aware of going forward."

"I'll take it on board. Let's finish this and get over to Cassandra's place."

"If she's in. She'll more than likely be at work at this time of day."

"True. Let's try and deal with that issue after, if we need to."

4

Laura's legs and backside were numb. In fact, her whole body ached from being stuck in the same position for hours on end. Her eyes stung with the tears she'd shed throughout the night. Peering up at the roof, through the gaps, she could tell it was daylight outside. Only glimpses of it, here and there, filled the barn, depressing her even more. She'd been alone for hours, possibly days. She had no concept of time, forced to go to the toilet where she sat. Fortunately, her body had only expelled urine up until now. She was dreading how she'd feel once the urge to have a number two hit her.

The man who'd abducted her hadn't been seen since, meaning basic necessities like food and water hadn't passed her lips since her arrival. She was all cried out now. What was the point in feeling sorry for herself? Why had he taken her and dumped her in this hellhole? What had she ever done to him? She hadn't recognised him, he was no one she knew, at least, she didn't think so. He'd said nothing about why she was here.

Halfway through the night, she'd dropped off to sleep, only to be woken by a dog howling in the distance, or could it have been a wolf? No, impossible, there were no wolves out here, not to her knowledge anyway. All she wanted, no, *needed*, were answers. How could she put things right without having an inkling why she was being punished like this?

Too many questions filled her mind and not enough answers or solutions as to how she was going to get out of this situation.

What had she done to someone to make them want to treat her this way?

The need to keep her here, tied up like an animal in the dark. None of it made sense to her. Yes, she'd done things in her past which she'd often regretted, however, none of them warranted someone treating her this way.

Life was all about learning from the mistakes you made, wasn't it? At least, that was her belief.

Thoughts of her parents drifted into her mind. She loved her mother deeply. Her father was a different matter. She'd held a grudge against him most of her life for deserting her as a child, although, saying that, her stepfather had more than filled his shoes over the years. Blood was thicker than water, she knew that, hence why she'd remained in contact with her real father during her childhood. Her mother hadn't always agreed with that, especially when he failed to show up for her birthday or at Christmas. Was that a man thing? Or a deliberate act? She'd never managed to get to the bottom of that one. All she wanted was to have her father in her life, rightly or wrongly in her mother's eyes. It had caused problems between them as she'd got older, and she'd tried to see more of her father once she was sixteen.

She had problems reassuring her mother that it wouldn't affect their relationship at all. Her mother refused to listen and often slated her father, bringing up the past when all Laura wanted to do was bury it and move on. But things had got worse between all three of them lately, so much so that...

A car.

Shit! He's back. Why? To bring me food and water? I hope so. My throat is raw, and my tummy is sore from hunger after barely eating yesterday.

The door to the barn opened. The daylight blinded her; all she could see was the outline of the man who'd dumped her here. He had something in his hand. She struggled to make out what it was. He walked slowly towards her.

"Please, why are you doing this?"

"I told you to keep your mouth shut." He stopped inches in front of her and slapped her face with enough force to jar her neck.

She faced him again, on the verge of tears, and stared at him.

He threw something on the floor, just out of reach. She lowered her head to take a look and then stared back at him.

It was a plate of food which had spilled onto the floor and into the straw beneath. How the hell was she supposed to eat that?

He sneered until an evil laugh took its place. "Don't say I don't feed you. Enjoy."

Tears brimmed, and her heart felt heavy. "Please, I need water."

"It's in your food. Hurry now, eat it quickly before it sinks in."

He turned and walked away. Using the daylight, she homed in on the food—it was just out of reach. She tugged on the chain wrapped around her core; it restricted her movement. He'd deliberately dropped the food where it lay to tease her. No, to torture her, that was her guess. *How long can I last without food and water? Days? Weeks? I won't be able to stand that. I hope I die soon. Please, God, don't let me suffer, allow me to go like this. Take me now.*

"Please," she called out.

The door to the barn slammed shut, and what sounded like a padlock was attached again.

Laura spent the next hour or so sobbing, until exhaustion took over and she finally dozed off.

5

"Where do you think we should go first?" Carla asked.

"Actually, I know I said I wanted to see her friend next, but something is niggling me about Andy. My heart is telling me one thing and my head another on this one. The pub is close by, isn't it?"

Carla nodded.

"Let's drop in there and see what the landlord has to say first and then move on to Cassandra Wells. Don't ask me why, but I think it's the way we should go, for now."

"Either way, both of them have to be questioned. Which way round we do it, shouldn't really matter. We're more likely to find the pub open than Cassandra at home."

"You're right, that settles it then. Sup up."

They drained their cups and left the café. The Three Feathers was a short distance away. It only took Sara two minutes to drive to the location. The car park was littered with another five vehicles.

"Not too busy. Let's hope the landlord can give us what we need."

They entered the public bar to find a tall, bearded man in his late thirties pulling a pint for a customer. The barman bobbed his head to acknowledge them, took the money from the customer and then moved to the end of the bar to speak with them.

"Morning, ladies, what can I get for you?"

Sara and Carla produced their IDs.

"DI Sara Ramsey and DS Carla Jameson. Are you the landlord, sir?"

"I am. Something wrong?"

"Would it be possible to have a brief chat with you?"

"I've got staff out back just coming on shift. If you can wait five minutes, I'm all yours."

"Excellent. We'll be seated in the booth over there." Sara pointed to a table tucked away at the rear of the pub.

"Can I get you a drink while you wait, on the house?"

"Thanks for the offer, but we'll decline, if it's all the same. We've not long had a coffee elsewhere."

"As you wish. Two ticks, and I'll be with you."

They settled into their seats, and not long after, the landlord joined them.

"I'm Jed, by the way."

Sara smiled as the man took a seat opposite them. "Pleased to meet you, Jed."

"Okay, I'm going to come right out and ask what this is all about."

"Don't worry, we're only making general enquiries."

He relaxed back against the wooden panel of the booth. "Phew, that's a relief. I hate it when your lot walk in, always feel guilty, even though I ain't done nothing wrong. Been like that all my life, you know, at school during assembly when the head used to demand who'd graffitied the boys' loos, I always coloured up, feeling guilty, even though I was bloody innocent. Sorry, I'm chuntering on. I'm known for it around these parts. What can I do for you?"

"There's no need to apologise, and no, you haven't done anything wrong. As I said, it's simply a general enquiry regarding one of your customers."

"I see. Which one in particular?"

"Andy Palmer?"

He frowned. "I know him. Been up to no good, has he?"

"That's what we're trying to find out. He gave us an alibi for his whereabouts on Tuesday night. Told us he was in here all night. Can you verify that?"

"I could if I was around. Hang on. Chris, here a sec." He gestured for a younger man who'd replaced him behind the bar to join him.

"Boss?"

"These nice young ladies are with the police. They want to know if Andy Palmer was in here Tuesday night. Was he? Now think carefully, lad."

"Yeah, he was in here all night, making the most of his girlfriend working, he told me."

"Interesting. I don't suppose you know what time he left, do you?" Sara asked.

"Around eleven. Drunk as a skunk he was. His mates had to call him a taxi to get home."

"That's brilliant. Thanks so much, Chris," Jed replied.

"Anything else?" Chris asked.

Sara shook her head. "That's all, thanks for your help."

Jed waited for his member of staff to walk out of earshot then leaned forward and asked, "What's the lad supposed to have done? I know he's got a record but I've kept an eye on him since he came out and never had any bother. Well, apart from the one incident…"

Sara's interest piqued. "Don't stop there, go on?"

"Me and my big mouth. All right, but you ain't heard this from me. I had to slap him down for being too friendly with one of the barmaids. She told me he touched her up on the way to the loo."

"Did you tackle him about it, Jed?"

"Yes and no. It was a difficult one. The girl had a bit of a reputation, you see. Always tough to accuse someone in that case, right?"

"Was the girl okay about that?"

"Not really, she left not long after."

"Because of the incident?"

"I don't think so. She was a troublemaker. I couldn't prove anything, but money was always missing when she was on shift, and bottles of booze, for that matter, too. Everything has been hunky-dory since she left. So make your own mind up about that. Some girls get a reputation for crying wolf, in my experience. It's so damn hard getting good staff these days," he added, lowering his voice.

"I can understand that. I don't suppose you have this girl's name and address, do you?"

"Can I ask why?"

"Again, just so we can tie up loose ends to our enquiry."

"I can get that for you. What's Andy done?"

"Nothing, as far as we know. Is he a regular?"

"Yep, since he came out, this has become his local."

"What about his girlfriend? Does she come in with him much?"

"I think I've seen her once or twice. I got the impression she hated coming here, too old-fashioned for her maybe. She seems nice enough, from the dealings I've had with her."

"When was the last time you saw her?"

Carla scribbled down some notes.

"About a month ago. Andy was his usual self, drunk as a skunk. He was all over her. She seemed pissed off with him and stormed out. He rushed out after her."

"Would you say he's keen on her then?"

"I don't get your question. They live together, so I guess they must be pretty close. Are you going to tell me what this is all about?"

"His girlfriend, Laura, has gone missing."

He slapped a hand on his forehead. "Whoa! When?"

"Tuesday night. Hence our need to know where Andy was."

"I get it now. Jesus, do you know what's happened to her?"

"Not really. It's an ongoing investigation. Her car was found abandoned close to her work. We've spoken to Andy this morning, and he appears to be holding up okay."

"Which means you're suspicious, right? If he isn't showing signs of being cut up about her."

"You're very astute, Jed. Let's just say the jury is still out for us. And we're not making our enquiries just because he has a record. We'd be doing the same, even if he didn't have one, fact."

"I agree. God, I hope she comes to light soon. Strange that her car was abandoned. You don't think she's in danger, do you?"

"The honest answer to that is, we don't know. So far, our enquiries have drawn a blank. One last question before we leave."

"I'm all ears."

"Since Andy has been a regular, has he fallen out with any of the other customers?"

"No, I don't believe so. You're thinking this is some kind of payback on him?"

Sara smiled. "You have a copper's brain, sir. I think you've missed your vocation in this life."

"My dad used to be a copper. We've had some interesting conversations over the years."

She tilted her head. "And you weren't tempted to join up at all?"

"At one time. I can't think what changed my mind…oh wait, yes, I can. Dad ended up in hospital because a bunch of thugs jumped him and his partner. They kicked the living daylights out of them both. Unfortunately, my dad's partner died after being in a coma for three months. Dad had a lucky escape. His injuries were so bad he was forced to give up work. Either that, or he could have taken on a desk job. That would have driven him nuts."

"Oh my, how awful. I'm so sorry to hear that. Is your father still alive?"

"He's hanging in there. Got a blood clot on the brain. He believes it's from where the thugs kicked his head all those years ago." Jed shrugged. "Who knows? I've never regretted my decision not to sign up. I love the career path I chose in the end. This place is a goldmine, even in uncertain times, you know, most pubs closing down through lack of trade."

"I'm glad the decision you took worked out well for you. If you can get me the barmaid's address, we'll leave you alone."

"Of course. Hang tight, I won't be long."

He left his seat and went back behind the bar. He returned within a few minutes and gave Sara a slip of paper with the name *Kerry Brett* and an address written on it.

"I appreciate this. Thanks for seeing us today."

"My pleasure. I hope Laura turns up safe and well soon." He leaned in and whispered, "Want me to keep an eye on Andy and report back to you?"

Sara lowered her voice. "That would be great. Here's my card."

He tucked it into his shirt pocket and saw them to the door. He shook their hands and then returned to the bar.

"Nice chap. The force missed out there," Sara noted outside the pub.

"Yeah. Maybe he'll come up trumps in the end and rethink his decision."

"Possibly. He seems pretty established here to me. Come on, that's two women we need to try and have a chat to now."

"Who first?"

"Let's go for Kerry."

"Any reason?"

They slipped into the car.

"No reason, maybe because I think it'll be a quicker visit. On the other hand, I could be talking a load of bullshit."

They both laughed.

Five minutes later, they arrived outside a small terraced house near the racecourse.

Sara rang the bell. "Did you hear it ring?"

Carla shook her head.

Sara knocked and then looked through the letterbox. A pair of legs suddenly came out of the front room. She stood quickly as the door opened.

"Yes, what do you want?" the spiky-haired blonde with Goth makeup asked.

"Hi, Kerry Brett?"

"No, she's still in bed, I'm her housemate. What do you want with her? She'll kill me if I wake her up and it's not important."

Sara showed her ID. "We're making general enquiries and wanted a quick chat, that's all."

The young woman wrinkled her nose. "Can't you come back when she's up?"

"When's that likely to be?"

"Your guess is as good as mine on that one. She didn't go to bed until five this morning."

"Sorry, we're not prepared to wait. Can you wake her up? We'll suffer the consequences."

"Not sure how you make that out. She's got a nasty temper. I'll be the one in the firing line, not you."

"Sorry, it's important we speak with her today."

"On your head then. *Kerry, the filth's here to see you*," she bellowed over her shoulder and smiled as she faced Sara and Carla again.

A groan came from upstairs, then a door slammed and another set of legs appeared and leisurely thumped down the stairs.

A brunette with tangled long hair and smudged makeup joined them at the door. "Filth? What do you want?"

"A chat, in private," Sara replied.

The other girl raised her hands and backed away. "All right, I'm out of here."

Sara waited until the girl who opened the door to them left the area completely and produced her warrant card for Kerry to study.

The woman peered briefly at it and asked, "What do you want? I ain't done nothing wrong."

"We're making enquiries that led us to The Three Feathers, and your name came up."

"What? I didn't do anything. Jed had it in for me from the word go. He couldn't wait for something to happen before he fired me."

"What happened?"

"That scum, Andy Palmer, copped a feel of my tit and denied it. Jed came down on his side and gave me the boot. He did it. Filthy dirt-bag, couldn't stand him having his hands on me. Why would I make something like that up?"

"Why weren't you prepared to stick up for yourself if your accusation was true?"

"Are you not listening? I told ya, Jed had it in for me. Money and bottles of booze going missing, and he suspected me. Once Andy put his spoke in, the writing was on the wall. I tried to put up some kind of defence, but he was having none of it."

"Sorry to hear that. Why did Andy touch you up?"

"How the fuck should I know? He's got a record, ain't he?"

"Were you aware of that record before he touched you?"

"Yes. I tried to steer clear of him, but he cornered me outside the ladies'. I slapped him and kneed him in the bollocks, that's probably why he reported me to Jed. I don't have to take that kind of shit from no man, no woman should."

"I agree. Surely, if you'd stood your ground Jed would have come out on your side eventually. He seemed a decent enough chap when we spoke to him."

"Ha! You're not listening to me. Oh, what's the point? I'm well shot of that place."

"Where are you working now?"

"I'm not. I'm on the dole because Jed wouldn't give me a proper reference. Without one of them, I ain't likely to find a decent job."

"Sorry to hear that. There must be some work you can do?"

"Nope. Hey, I ain't discussing my life with coppers so you guys can fit me up at a later date. What do you want with me?"

"We heard about the incident and needed to know what went on from your side. Have you either seen or heard from Andy since?"

"What? Why would I? As far as I'm concerned he's a tosser, out for what he can get. If he comes near me, I promise, I won't bloody hold back next time. I restrained myself last time."

"You call kneeing him in the bollocks restraining yourself?" Sara tried to make light of the situation, to relieve some of the tension in the air.

"Law against that? Oh wait, you're not trying to trick me here, are ya? You gonna slam me with an assault charge to add to the other shit I've been through?"

"No. I swear. If what you're telling us really happened the way it did then I wouldn't blame you in the slightest for doing what you did. No man should come on that heavily with a woman."

"Glad you're on my side. Does that mean I can lay a charge on him?"

Sara shrugged. "I can't sway your decision either way, however, if you're out of work and unable to find a job because of the incident, then it might be worth you considering going to a tribunal with a claim."

Kerry chewed her lip. "I'll think about it. On the flip side, I suppose I'd rather let things go, not that it's going to do me much good doing that."

"Think it over. Do you know anyone else who had a problem with Andy at the pub? Other staff members or customers maybe?"

She paused to mull over the question and shook her head. "Nope, I don't think so. Only me. If I'd heard of anyone else, I probably would have kicked up a major fuss about him. You know what men are like, they tend to stand up for each other. In Jed's eyes, he's a good punter, spends a lot of dosh there, so I suppose he wanted to keep Andy onside. Ugh…just saying that man's name leaves a bitter taste in my mouth. Look, my take is that if he tried it on with me, there will be others out there who have had to deal with the same shit. He's a convicted rapist, right? That's a fact he can't deny."

"I hear you. We'll definitely do some extra digging on him. Thanks for speaking with us today. Sorry to have disturbed your sleep."

"Don't worry about it. I missed out on breakfast. I'll have that then go back to bed. It's not as if I have anything else to get up for, is it?"

"Before we go, did you ever meet Andy's girlfriend?"

"Yeah, once or twice. What about her?"

"She's gone missing. That's what we're investigating."

"Whoa, no shit! Well, I'm not surprised. I'd keep my eye on that bastard, that's all I can say."

"Thanks for your advice. We intend to."

Kerry shut the door.

"Interesting conversation," Carla said on their way back to the car.

"Very. Let's sit on it for now and see what the friend has to say before we head back to the station."

"If she's in."

Sara grinned. "Well, we've been damned lucky so far. Fingers crossed our luck doesn't run out."

Flat three turned out to be at the very top of a high-rise tower. "Thank God the lift is working. I didn't relish having to walk up fifteen flights of stairs."

Carla smiled. "I'll echo that sentiment."

Cassandra Wells opened the door to the flat looking dishevelled. *Bloody hell! What is it with people these days? Don't they ever get up at the normal time?*

Wiping the crusty sleep out of her eye, Cassandra shielded her face against the daylight. "Yes?"

Sara and Carla showed their IDs then Sara said, "Would it be all right if we came in and spoke to you?"

"Do you have to? Can't you say what you've got to tell me here and bugger off? The place is a tip. I had a party last night to celebrate my birthday."

"Belated happy birthday. It'd be better if we came inside."

She huffed out a breath and threw back the door which promptly hit the internal wall behind it. "If you must. Go in the lounge, that room there. I need to put the kettle on for a coffee. I guess I'd better offer you a drink."

"You don't have to do that on our part. We're fine."

Cassandra carried on walking up the narrow hallway. "Okay, I won't be a sec. I need one, it feels like my effing throat has been cut."

They entered the lounge. Cassandra was right, it was a tip. There was a clothes horse in front of the small window which was filling the air with a damp smell. Plus, every surface, including all the chairs, was covered in either balloons or wrapping paper. In the corner was a pile of gifts.

"Popular girl," Sara muttered, pointing at the presents.

"So it would seem."

THE LIES SHE TOLD

Footsteps sounded in the hallway, and a door opened. Voices filtered out of another room.

"There's someone else here," Sara announced in a hushed voice.

The door opened, and Cassandra entered with a steaming mug in her hand. "Shit, I didn't realise it was that messy in here. I did warn you. Here, take a seat." She swept her hand across the couch, throwing the contents onto the floor. She did the same with the easy chair and dropped into it.

After settling onto the couch, Carla took out her notebook, and Sara started asking questions.

"First of all, thank you for agreeing to see us today. Sorry if it's an inconvenience to you."

"I won't know that until you tell me what this is about."

"We're making enquiries into an incident which occurred a few days ago."

"Oh right. What type of incident? Wait, let me say that if it happened last night then I was here with at least twenty other people."

"Good to know. No, I said the incident happened a few nights ago, on Tuesday. We're not here to interrogate you about what happened, more to ask questions about who the incident happened to, really."

Cassandra's brow wrinkled. "Umm...my head must be foggier than I first thought. Do you want to run that past me again?"

"Sorry, my fault entirely. Okay, what we want to know is when you last saw Laura Tyler."

Cassandra took a sip from her mug and sat back. "Before I answer that, I want to know why you're asking."

"I'd like you to answer my question first."

The door opened again, and a youngish man in jeans and a sweater entered the room. He had a mug in his right hand. He nodded, said a weak *hello* and headed towards Cassandra's chair and perched on the arm.

"This is my fella, Sam. I asked him to join us, I hope that's okay?"

"Fine. Hi, Sam. Bear with us, we only have a few questions to ask. Laura Tyler, when was the last time you saw her, Cassandra?"

The couple shared a quizzical look. Cassandra shifted uncomfortably which sent warning signs to Sara.

"A few months ago."

"Can you be more specific?"

"Around Christmas, if you must know."

Sara picked up on the anger in Cassandra's tone. "Why say it like that, Cassandra? Is there something you need to tell me?"

"Like what?"

"You tell me. I asked if you've seen your supposed best friend lately, and your face and tone turned sour. Why?"

Another sip of her drink meant that Cassandra had time to contemplate her answer. Sara wasn't getting a good feeling about this visit.

"All right. We fell out around then."

"Ah, that's better. May I ask why?"

Again, the couple glanced at each other. This time their gazes didn't hold for any length of time.

"Cassandra? Sam? Is someone going to tell me what's going on here? Why did you fall out with your best friend?"

"It really doesn't matter any more. I'm past it, we all are."

"No, that's not good enough. You've raised a subject which I'm interested in and could help our case, so please, do me the courtesy of telling me what went on between you."

"You need to tell me why you're here first. You haven't told me what this visit is about, and judging by your tone and offhand attitude, I think I have a right to know."

"Okay, Laura went missing on Tuesday night."

Cassandra gasped and clutched her boyfriend's hand. "What? Missing where? How? Hang on, why come here? You don't think I've got anything to do with this, do you?"

"No, that's not why we came. We were told that you're Laura's best friend. All we wanted to know was when you last saw her."

"It was just after Christmas." Her voice dipped. "Just after it happened…"

"What was that?" Sara strained her neck to hear.

Another sip of her coffee, and Cassandra said, "I don't want to talk about it."

"That's entirely up to you, of course, but it really doesn't help our case. As well as trying to find where Laura is, we're also interested in learning what type of character she is. If there's something you think we should know, please, just tell us. Has she got involved in something dangerous, is that what you're suggesting?"

"No, nothing like that." Again, Cassandra appeared uncomfortable and shifted back and forth in her seat.

"You're going to have to tell her now you've opened your big mouth," Sam muttered.

Cassandra glared at him and snapped, "I don't want every Tom, Dick and Harry knowing our business."

"If it's important and I find out that you were intentionally keeping it from us, then you could get yourself in bother. It's always better to be upfront with us during an investigation. It'll prevent us from wasting our valuable time. So…what is it you want to tell us?" Sara urged.

Cassandra stared into her mug, then she took a sip and sighed. "I caught her in bed with him."

"Him? Who? Oh my, not you, Sam, is that what you're saying?"

Cassandra lifted her head. Large tears bulged and dripped onto her puffy cheeks. "Yes, they were both at it behind my back."

"Okay, I can tell this is a sensitive issue. Would you prefer to discuss this alone?"

"No, he can stay. Let him see how much he destroyed me and my friendship with Laura."

"I'm sorry to hear that, Cassandra. One question, why did you forgive your boyfriend and not your best friend?"

"It worked out that way."

"Whose decision was it to break up? Yours or hers?"

"Hers in the end. She couldn't believe that I could forgive him. I was willing to forgive both of them but…shit, it was such a mess. At the time I wanted to dump them both. How do you move on with your

M A COMLEY

life when the two people who you care most about have deceived you in the harshest way?"

"How indeed? But you managed it."

"I had to dig deep to forgive them. I offered her the olive branch, and she refused to accept it. Sam was different. You'll have to ask him why he did it, he refuses to tell me."

Sara raised an eyebrow at the boyfriend. "Care to tell us?"

He heaved out a sigh and threw his head back. "Why? Why bring it up again now? We were getting along fine together, Cas. Opening up old wounds could be disastrous for us."

Cassandra shrugged. "Tell her. We'll discuss it later, after they've gone."

"Bloody hell. All right, in a moment of weakness, Laura managed to come on to me. She'd always been flirty with me. Cas was working late one night; Laura came round to see her. I told her she wouldn't be back for hours, but Laura insisted on waiting for her to come home. I felt awkward denying her access to the flat so let her in. We started chatting, I offered Laura a coffee, but she said she wanted a glass of wine instead, then she asked for a drop of brandy, and one thing led to another and…"

"They ended up in bed," Cassandra finished for him.

Sara shook her head. "That's a regrettable situation. You must count yourself lucky that Cassandra didn't kick you out, Sam?"

"I do. We went through a rough patch, but we've come out the other end. We're now stronger than ever, at least we were, until you showed up and started digging."

"As I said, we're dealing with an important investigation. Do you have any idea where Laura might have gone, either of you?"

They both shook their heads, their expressions nonplussed.

"No. How could we, if we haven't laid eyes on her in nearly two months?" Cassandra eventually said.

"Okay, before you guys split up, did she ever give you any indication where she might go if things got bad around here? That sort of thing would really help us. Time's getting on, and she's still missing."

"No, although, have you tried her father? He used to live up in

Cumbria, you know, the Lake District. She used to tell me how much she loved it up there. It gave her time to reflect. What's that no-mark of a boyfriend said?"

"No, we've yet to contact her father, we'll get on to that today. As for Andy, he's bearing up, shall we say."

"Bearing up? He's not upset? That bloody figures. It's all about him and no one else matters. I wouldn't be surprised if he did have something to do with her going missing."

"You think he might have harmed her?"

Cassandra shrugged. "I wouldn't put it past him. I warned her about going out with a bloody *rapist*."

"She was aware of his record then? That much we haven't managed to establish. Her parents mentioned he was an ex-con but couldn't tell us what he was put away for."

"Yes, she thought it was funny. I told her how warped she was. I suppose that's when our relationship began to falter. When she first introduced us, he was all smiles. Sam will back me up here, won't you? After a month or so he was more demanding of her time which meant she didn't have time for me."

"And yet she came here and…well, you know, with Sam."

"Yeah, I know. It confused the hell out of me at the time, too, that's why I went ballistic. Oh, I don't know. She was bang out of order, either way. Saying that, I haven't got a clue where she is. You should be asking him that. Oh God, what if he's done away with her, you know, killed her?"

Sara rubbed at her chin with her finger and thumb. "It's an avenue we're looking into. Any help you can give us will be beneficial to the case. How would you perceive their relationship?"

Cassandra glanced out of the window and then back at Sara. "She was a closed shop on that front, refused to let me in. I tried to find out if she was happy with him. On several occasions she told me to mind my own business."

"And that's how she thanked you for being concerned, by sleeping with your boyfriend?"

"Exactly. I'm still trying to figure out what I did so wrong in her eyes to deserve her treating me like that."

"Sam, did Laura ever confide in you?"

"Go on, say it, between the sheets?" Sam added sarcastically.

Sara shrugged. "If you want to add that, it's fine by me."

"No, we never discussed him, which at the time I thought was odd."

"How many times did you sleep with her?" Sara pushed her luck.

"Jesus! Just the one. My bad, it was the biggest mistake of my life so far, shoot me for it. I still feel bad. Thankfully, Cassandra has been great about it and has been a treasure forgiving me. She knows I'll never do anything like that again. Right, hon?"

"I think so," Cassandra said uncertainly.

"So, what about other friends, did Laura have any?"

Cassandra grunted. "A few, she wasn't really one for having a lot of friends, not really. Which is another reason why I found things difficult to comprehend. I was virtually her only friend and yet, look how she frigging treated me. I've questioned my loyalty to her ever since, if I'm honest. I've had time to reflect on our relationship and what each of us gave to it, and surprise, surprise, I came out on top each and every time. She's definitely one of life's takers, not givers. Always late wishing me a happy birthday or handing over Christmas presents every year. Thinking back, I should have dumped her long ago."

"Sorry to hear that. It's sad when people are so selfish. Can you recall her getting into bother at all? Either personally or at work perhaps?"

"Plenty of times at work over the years. Although, she's keen on the job she has now, keener on her boss I think than the work she does."

Sara tilted her head with interest. "Are you telling me she has a crush on Neil Armitage?"

Cassandra snorted. "Crush? I'd say she has the hots for him. Look, I know you're going to think this is me being bitter, but I'm over what happened and only telling you the truth. I should've listened to my gut about her and steered clear." She jabbed Sam in the shoulder. "I should've told him to do the same, too. Or at least made him aware of what a maneater she was."

"Er…ya think?" Sam shouted back.

"All right, let's not revisit that, try and remain calm. Cassandra, can you tell me where she worked prior to the college?"

"Yep, NatWest bank in Hereford."

Carla jotted the information down.

"Thanks, maybe we'll drop by and see what we can find out."

"The manager is Stewart Joyston, he's the one you need to speak to. Things got a little hot between them too."

"Okay. We'll do some digging about that. What about her previous employers, can you help there?"

"Sorry, no. I wish I could."

"Not to worry. We'll do some digging, see what we can come up with. What about previous boyfriends, anything there?"

"I don't know, hang on…nope, I can't think of anyone."

"Okay, we're going to leave things there unless you have anything else you think we should know?"

"I can't think of anything, can you, Sam?"

He shook his head in response and added, "We hope you find her soon."

Cassandra showed them to the front door. Sara said, "Sorry if my questions have hampered you guys getting along. It was all necessary, I assure you."

"Don't mention it. We'll be fine. It doesn't hurt to bring up the past now and again to keep him in line."

"Oi, you, I am here, you know."

Cassandra winked at him. "You think I'm stupid. Don't answer that." She faced Sara. "Can you give me your phone number, just in case Laura shows up here?"

"Of course. Here you go." Sara handed her a card. "If you think of anything else important, just give me a tinkle."

"I'll do that."

They left the flat and hopped in the lift.

"What did you make of them?" Carla flipped through the notes she'd taken.

"Another time when the jury is out. My mind flicked between different scenarios. At one time I felt sorry for the couple, the next I thought they could be behind her disappearance as some kind of payback…"

"Come the end?" Carla pushed.

"My final thought is that Laura isn't coming across too well with anyone we've questioned. I'm also frigging livid with her boss for not telling us that there was something going on between them."

"That's not been established yet, 'the crush' might not have led anywhere. Maybe he felt uncomfortable with all the attention and that's why he didn't bother telling us."

"Possibly. The thing that gets to me is why people are refusing to tell the truth. I'm also not getting the best of feelings about Andy either. Discounting his record, that's not what I'm getting at here, well, what if…?"

"What if he spoke to other prisoners and has upped his ante? Taken to killing women, is that where you were heading?"

Sara raised her hands and turned them upwards. "I don't have all the answers. Yes, it might be that, but there's also something else to consider here. What if he got in with the wrong crowd in prison and they asked him to do things for them on the outside and he's gone against that? What if the man at the top has taken Laura and is holding her as some kind of ransom?"

"I'd say you've been reading too many crime novels." Carla giggled.

"I think you might be right. Another reason why we should stick with the facts and not let our minds and hearts run away from us. Let's get back to base. Have a breather from questioning folks for now."

6

Back at the station, Sara sat behind her desk and went over her notes. A light knock on the door interrupted her. She looked up to see DCI Price peering around the door.

"All right if I come in?"

She gestured for her boss to join her. "Of course, anything wrong?"

"No. I told the desk sergeant to ring me as soon as you got back. I've been on tenterhooks all morning. How's it going?"

Sara leaned back and blew out an exasperated breath. "I guess I need to ask how well you know Laura Tyler."

"Oh God, *not well* would be my initial answer. She's the daughter of my friend, and that about sums it up. Why?"

"The more we're finding out about her, the more my hackles are rising."

"Shit! Like what?" Carol linked her hands across her flat stomach.

"Off the record…I think the term would be 'maneater'. Seems to me her morals are as loose as…well, you get the picture. Sorry if that causes offence, boss, but I'd rather be upfront from the outset."

"Inspector, are you telling me you think she was likely abducted because of her character?"

"I'm telling you it possibly added to the outcome, yes. This morning, Carla and I have been out there talking to all the main people in her life and, apart from her parents, no one has—no, that's wrong—only a few of them had a kind word to say about her."

"Oh my. I wonder if Lin realises."

"I don't know, and I'd rather not be the one to tell her, if I'm honest. We're going to keep digging obviously, but I have to warn you the signs aren't good, not from what we've learnt so far."

"Who have you spoken to?"

"Her boss, her boyfriend and her *former* best friend, they're the significant players in this. It's my intention to go over the case with the team in a little while. They've been gathering information for us while Carla and I have been out there. You're welcome to sit in."

"I'd like that, thanks. I'm devastated by what you've told me. Wait, you mentioned you had spoken to her *former* best friend. Are you going to tell me what she said?"

"In a nutshell, Laura slept with this girl's boyfriend."

"What? Holy crapioli! What about the others? Have they said similar?"

"Not really. The boss seemed friendly enough. Her best friend admitted there was something going on between them, even though he didn't tell us."

Carol shook her head and seemed mortified. "So, what do you think has happened to her?"

"Can I save that for the meeting? I hate having to repeat myself. Come on, I'd like to start now."

"Okay. I don't suppose you've got any brandy in that desk of yours, have you?"

"Nope, sorry, even if I did have a secret stash, I'm hardly likely to tell my boss, am I?" Sara winked, and together they left the room.

She clapped to draw everyone's attention. "Team, we need to go over what we've discovered so far, and yes, DCI Price is going to sit in on the meeting. Don't let that influence what you need to say. She wants to hear the truth about what we've uncovered, okay?"

The team all nodded and pulled their chairs into position. In her absence, Carla had transferred some of her notes onto the whiteboard, as agreed.

Sara briefly cast her attention over the board and then stood beside it. She ran through what they'd experienced with those they'd already spoken to. Now and again, she glanced in Carol's direction, her expression never altering; she still seemed baffled by what she'd heard.

"So, that's where we are. Now, it's your turn to tell me where you're up to. Who wants to start?"

Jill's hand rose. "I'm still trying to track down the father, no joy yet."

Sara raised a finger. "Carla, what did Cassandra Wells say about him?"

Her partner flicked though her notes. "He lives up in Cumbria, the Lake District, or so she thought."

Sara clicked her fingers. "That's right. Jill, maybe that will narrow it down a bit for you."

Jill jotted down the information. "I'll get on it right away, boss, well, after we've finished."

"Okay, so here's where we stand and my perception of things to date. I'm not holding back, the boss is already aware of what I think. As far as I'm concerned, Laura could have a few enemies out there, just because of how she's acted in the past. She's already damaged a perfectly good friendship with Cassandra Wells, her best friend, by sleeping with her boyfriend. By the way, Cassandra and Sam are still together, and yet she chose to break contact with Laura. That could be taken two ways, and I'm prepared to keep an open mind on the couple going forward."

"What if they plotted something between them?" Barry asked.

Sara shrugged. "I'm simply laying all the facts on the table right now. Her boss, Neil Armitage, also neglected to mention what Cassandra told us, that he and Laura were close. I feel we should pay him another visit and get the truth out of him either this afternoon or tomorrow. In the meantime, I'd like you, Marissa, to find out what his background is for me."

"Will do, boss."

"That leaves us with Andy. I might be speaking out of turn here but I think he has to be our main suspect. And yes, I'm sorry to say that I'm taking his record into consideration when I say that, because let's face it, that's all we have to work with so far. I'm aware he has a solid alibi, but there are two possibilities with him. We spoke to the landlord at the pub, and he assured us Andy was there all evening and went home in a taxi—he was paralytic. However, this morning we spoke to a former barmaid at the pub who Andy had tried it on with. That information alone has caused me great concern. He clearly hasn't mended his ways. Is he behind Laura's abduction? Or, the other possibility is that there's some sort of connection with prison. Did he get in with the wrong crowd and they've got a hold over him to do a job for them on the outside? Has he reneged on the deal and they've punished him by kidnapping Laura, holding her to ransom? I think we should contact the prison, see what we can find out about Andy Palmer and what he got up to on the inside. Craig, will you do that for me?"

"Of course I will, boss."

Carla's hand shot up to speak.

"Go on, Carla," Carol Price said.

"Well, I'm just adding a word of caution on the Andy front, only because he didn't seem that perturbed to me."

"About her going missing?" Price asked, her brow furrowed.

"Yeah, I know that doesn't make a lot of sense. What I'm trying to say is that if someone on the inside was pulling his strings, wouldn't he be freaking out? You know, if they had a dangerous hold over him?"

Sara nodded. "Maybe, and yes, I agree, while we were there, all he seemed intent on doing was eating his full English before it got cold. However, my gut is telling me not to trust him."

"Then I'm happy to go with your gut on this one, Inspector," Carol replied. "Anything else?"

"Not as yet. I don't think that's a bad morning's work so far. Carla and I need to go and have a chat with the ex-husband. I think the way forward is to really dig deep into Laura's past. Oh, yes, we've also got to question her former boss as well. Cassandra told us that things got a 'little hot' between them and that's why Laura left."

"Bloody hell. I'm not telling you how to suck eggs here, but when you speak to her mother, would you mind keeping quiet about some of this information? Otherwise it's going to tear her apart. I don't think she realises how tarnished her daughter's reputation is. Putting myself in her shoes, with Laura still missing, I truly wouldn't want to know. It would only add to my concern for her."

"Don't worry, I wasn't about to tell her anything we've uncovered. I'll keep it brief and to the point when I check in with her. I'm keen to contact her father, though, see what he has to say about her."

The meeting drew to a close, and DCI Price left them to it.

Sara exhaled the second she exited the room. "That was tough, going through all that while she was here."

Carla headed over to the vending machine and bought everyone a coffee. She handed them around and gave a cup to Sara then perched on the desk behind her. "What next? The ex-hubby, the ex-boss?"

"I'd like to hold off speaking to them until the morning, don't ask me why, maybe we just need to gather more information first before we tackle them."

"Maybe, otherwise you'll be asking the same old questions over and over. It becomes laborious then, doesn't it?"

"Ooo...get you using big words halfway through the day."

"Sod off. I do occasionally."

Sara raised her cup at her partner. "Cheers, I was only teasing. Anything to lighten the load. We've got very little to go on, and it's driving me potty. I'm not sure what direction we should be going in next."

"Why's that? Because the chief is involved? Is that a stumbling block on this one, do you think?"

"Truthfully, yes. I have to admit, it's not helpful in the slightest."

"You're going to have to put that out of your mind, if we're going to find Laura."

"Tell me something I don't know." She rubbed a hand across the back of her aching neck to ease out the tension knot which had developed.

"Boss, I think I have something which will cheer you up," Jill shouted across the room.

Sara rushed over to her desk. "Tell me you've located the father."

"I have an address and a phone number for you."

Sara patted Jill on the shoulder. "I knew I could count on you. Get him on the phone for me, Jill, I'll take it in the office."

She raced through and threw herself into her seat. The phone on her desk rang, and she whipped it out of the docking station.

"Boss, I have Mr Tyler on the line for you."

"Thanks, Jill." There was a click. "Hello, Mr Tyler?"

"Yes, that's me. What's this about?" His tone was one of confusion.

"Let me introduce myself first of all. I'm DI Sara Ramsey of the West Mercia Police, sir."

"Yeah, okay, I get that. I repeat, what's this about?"

"Your daughter, Laura." Silence filled the line. "Mr Tyler, are you still there?"

"I am. What about her?"

"Well, she was reported missing, and I wondered if she had contacted you within the last day or so."

"No. Missing? What's that supposed to mean, Inspector?"

"As in, no one within her immediate circle of family and friends has heard from her. She's gone off-grid, and we're trying to find her."

"I see. No, she hasn't contacted me, not recently anyway."

"May I ask when you last heard from her?"

"Around a month ago."

His answers were brief and to the point. Sara couldn't help wondering why. "Do you mind me asking what the conversation was about, sir?"

"General chitchat, amongst other things."

"Other things, such as?"

He tutted and sighed heavily. "Other things. Oh, I don't know why I said that. Just ignore me."

"Sir, if there's something I should know, please, please find it in your heart to tell me."

He fell silent and contemplated his answer for a while. "I don't know what you expect me to say. I certainly don't know why she's gone missing."

"If she was in trouble, would you tell me?"

"Yes, of course I would. I'm not that heartless, Inspector."

"That's not what I was inferring, sir. I get the impression you're holding something back from me. Are you?"

"My daughter and I have what you'd probably describe as an off-on relationship, more off than on. She usually only contacts me when she wants something from me."

"I'm sorry to hear that, sir. May I ask why she got in touch the last time you heard from her?"

"It's usually about money."

"She wanted money off you?"

"That's correct. She knows I don't have a lot. I've been medically retired for five years, and funds are quite low, shall we say?"

"That's a shame. Sorry, sir."

"I didn't mention it to gain any sympathy from you."

"Did she tell you what the money was for?"

"No. Said she was in some kind of trouble. I tried to get it out of her, but she refused to tell me, therefore, I refused to help her."

Shit! Well, that's not very helpful, either for the investigation or for Laura.

"Because you didn't have the funds?"

"No, more on principle than anything else. She's got a job, I haven't. If she and that mongrel of a boyfriend of hers choose to spend all their money on booze then...well, that's up to them, she shouldn't expect me to bail them out. I know he put her up to it. He's a bad 'un, that one, she shouldn't have got involved with the fecker."

"Have you met him?"

"No. I've stayed well clear of them since she took up with him. What's he had to say about her disappearance?"

"Nothing much, if I'm honest. He was on a night out when she went missing."

"See, I bloody rest my case. I'd like to have the money to go out socialising as much as they do. They shouldn't expect other family members to foot the bill for them."

"I agree, sir."

"Good, I know I'm right. Youngsters today need to get their priorities in order. Maybe it's the world to blame, they're able to get loans and mortgages at the drop of a hat. When I was starting out, a mortgage was only achievable if you had a decent income. Now they're dishing them out like bloody Jelly Babies. Giving the youngsters the wrong impression. If they can't afford something they want, they need to save up for it, like we had to in days gone by. Damn, I sound like my ruddy mother now. Good job I didn't live through the Second World War, you'd never get me off the phone."

Sara chuckled. "You're not telling me anything new, I've had this discussion over and over with both my parents and my grandparents. It's definitely a different world we're living in today, that's for sure. May I ask how things were left between you, sir?"

"They were frosty, to say the least. Even if I had the money in the bank, I wouldn't have handed it over on principle. She needs to stand on her own two feet at some time. The trouble is, that mother of hers spoils her rotten."

"May I ask why Laura didn't go to her mother for financial help?"

"She did. This time her mother, or rather her stepfather, put his foot down and sent her packing, hence her coming to me cap in hand. I felt bad for turning my back on her but I think I was in the right. They have to understand the value of money if they're going to make anything of their lives."

"I couldn't agree more. Are you sure you haven't heard from her in the last month?"

"Categorically, no. Has something happened to her, or are you telling me she's just gone AWOL?"

"We're unsure yet. We've questioned several people, and no one has seen or heard from her since Tuesday evening."

"I didn't think the police had the time to spend on missing people these days. How come you're involved?"

"Your ex-wife is friends with my DCI, and she asked me to look into the case, to try and get Laura back home as soon as possible."

"I see, you're telling me it pays to have friends in high places, eh? Good old Lin, I knew she'd have a use one day. Sorry, that was uncalled for. I don't usually go out of my way to bad-mouth my ex-wife. I tend to leave the past where it belongs, buried deep and untouched, never to be revisited."

"We all have one. May I ask what went wrong between you?"

"We grew apart. It's been years since we parted, and no, don't ask me to give you a definite figure on that either."

Sara smiled. "Okay, I won't ask. Look, if Laura does get in touch with you, will you promise to contact me?"

"If I must. My guess is she'll turn to everyone else before she comes knocking on my door. I hope you find her soon. Will you keep me informed?"

"I can't promise to do that, sir, it might cause friction between Laura's mother and myself. Feel free to ring me at any time, though, to enquire how the case is progressing."

"Thank you, Inspector, I'll be sure to do that. In the meantime, I'll hold my daughter in my thoughts and hope that nothing bad has happened to her."

"Thank you for speaking with me, Mr Tyler."

"Not a problem. Goodbye, Inspector."

Sara replaced the phone in its docking station and sat back. Her gaze drifted towards the window. The clouds ambled by as she reflected on the conversation she'd just had with Laura's father.

Carla popped her head into the office. "How did you get on? Has he seen or heard from her?"

"Nope. No further forward."

"Why do you look perplexed?" Carla sat in the chair opposite her.

Sara tutted. "You know when you speak to someone and you don't know what to make of their reaction to something you've said? Well, that's how I'm feeling right now."

"As in, you think he's hiding something?"

"I don't frigging know. Christ, give me an effing gruesome murder case to solve any day, rather than a sodding missing person case that is driving me to distraction. Do you know what's truly eating away at me?"

"No, but there's clearly something, you're not your usual bubbly self, that's for sure."

Sara rolled her eyes. "I'm not sure 'bubbly self' could ever be used to describe me, love. Anyway, it's the fact that no one seems to have a good word to say about Laura, that's truly ticking me off."

"No one? Or is that you stretching the truth a little? What about her parents?"

"Okay, my mistake. See, I told you, this is messing with my head, and we've got a few more people to question yet."

"Maybe they'll be able to point us in the right direction. You want to hear what I think?"

"Go on, you know I always expect you to speak freely."

"I think someone has kidnapped her either to punish her or to punish a loved one. I'm not a hundred percent sure which option to choose."

"Helpful." Sara grinned. "If it's the latter, we're back to Andy possibly being in the spotlight again, right?"

Carla shrugged. "Who bloody knows? I've got Craig chasing that. The last I heard he was waiting for the governor to come out of an important meeting with his boss."

"Good. I'm mentally bushed, but I think we should get out there and speak to at least her former boss before we call it a day."

Carla checked the time on her watch. "It's coming up to three now."

"I thought it was around that, enough time to interview her former boss. I'm fed up with being the nice guy. I think I should go on in there and, well, demand the answers."

Carla's head bobbed from side to side. "Maybe. It's not always the correct way of doing things, though, is it?"

"You're telling me to keep my frustration reined in."

Carla smiled and left the room. Sara joined her in the incident room moments later.

7

The NatWest was reasonably busy. Sara walked up to the girl at the reception desk and produced her ID. "Hi, I'd like to see Mr Joyston, if that's possible."

"I'll see if he's available. I'll be right back."

"Thanks."

They waited in silence until the young blonde woman returned. "He's just finished with a customer and said he can spare you five or ten minutes, if that's enough for you. He's expecting another customer in fifteen minutes."

"That should be enough time."

They followed the woman through a security door and along a carpeted hallway to a room at the back. The woman walked straight into the room and gestured for Sara and Carla to join her. She made the introductions and closed the door behind her after she departed.

"Thank you for agreeing to see us, Mr Joyston," Sara said, ignoring what she told Carla about going in heavy-handed.

"My pleasure. Marie didn't tell me what this is about."

"We're investigating a case, and your name cropped up. So we thought we'd drop by and ask you a few questions, if that's all right?"

"I try to do my bit for the community, feel free. What case, may I ask?"

"It's a missing person case."

He raised an eyebrow. "Are you going to tell me who's missing?"

Sara studied him carefully to assess his reaction. "Laura Tyler."

He frowned and fidgeted in his chair. "I see."

"I see, as in, you remember her?"

"Yes, of course I remember her. She was my secretary up until last year. I don't think my memory is that bad, Inspector."

"Good. Have you heard from her since she left?"

"No, nothing at all. Her final wages went through head office straight into her bank account, so there was no need for her to step foot in this building again."

Sara picked up on the sharp edge to his tone. "Why did she leave, Mr Joyston? Maybe you can enlighten us there."

"She was a pest. She didn't start out that way. The first few months she was eager to please, workwise, I mean."

"What changed?"

He sighed and puffed out his cheeks. "Quite frankly, she did."

"In what way?"

"I don't know really. Well, I do, but it's hard to fathom. All I can tell you is that one day she was happy to keep her distance, the next she appeared to be all over me. And no, that's not my bloody ego speaking either. I did nothing at all to lead her on, I swear."

"Did she give you any indication why she changed so rapidly?"

"No, nothing at all. Maybe I'm at fault a little. At first, I thought she'd settled into her job and her flirtatious nature had emerged. But it soon became apparent that it had gone further than that."

"Really? In what way?"

"In a sexual harassment kind of way. I've never felt so uncomfortable around a colleague before then. I keep thinking back to the beginning, when she first began working for me to see if the signs were there. I don't think I encouraged her. It's tough knowing where to draw the line with a staff member. You can ask any of my previous secretaries, and they've never had a problem with me."

THE LIES SHE TOLD

"You're saying that she sexually harassed you and not the other way around?"

"Absolutely, it was that way round. I'm an engaged man and love my fiancée dearly. I would never dream of cheating on her. I'm also dedicated to my work and would never put that in jeopardy by having a sordid fling. You have to believe me."

"Only we were under the impression you had the hots for each other."

His mouth opened and closed, mimicking a fish out of water, but no words came out. Finally, he spluttered, "I can categorically deny that. She might have 'had the hots' for me, but it definitely wasn't reciprocated, I can assure you. Jesus, to think she's told people that. Well, all that does is prove I was right to end her employment with this bank. Good Lord." Beads of sweat broke out on his forehead.

"Okay, let's calm down, Mr Joyston."

"Calm down? To think I've been lied about in such a way by that… that woman, has incensed me beyond belief, I can tell you. How would you react if someone turned an incident upside down on its head like she has?" His cheeks flared up in anger. He picked up a pen and jabbed it on his desk blotter as if to calm his rage.

"I'm sorry. We find this all the time during an investigation, people discovering things about someone they worked with which turned out to be either false or malicious. While she was working here, did Laura ever confide in you?"

"About what?" he asked, a tad calmer.

"I don't know, about her personal life. Was she with her boyfriend then? Andy Palmer?"

"No, that name doesn't ring a bell. She was single while she worked here, or so she told me. Who knows if that was the truth or not after the lies she told? I'm lucky I have an exemplary record with the bank and have turned this branch around during my time here, otherwise I believe I would have been fired by now, thanks to that bitch. I'm sorry to resort to name-calling, but seriously, that girl has got a screw loose, for want of a better phrase, I swear it on my life. To flip like that…she can't be all there."

Sara's heart went out to the man. She could tell how uncomfortable this conversation was making him feel, judging by the sweat pouring off him. "How did her behaviour manifest itself?"

His head dipped a little, along with his voice. "I asked her to come in one day, to take some notes down for a letter I wanted to send to head office. She started flashing her legs at me. I remember she had on a skirt which had a huge split up the side. Obviously, my eyes were drawn to her lower half. She made the most of that, opening her legs, showing me more, if you like."

"And you didn't think to look away or reprimand her in any way?"

"No, it never crossed my mind it would escalate so quickly. Within a few days, her blatant attempt to flaunt herself had turned into a full-on attack on all my senses. I did my best to ignore her, but do you realise how difficult that became when we're supposed to work alongside each other?" He stared off to the left and then shook his head. "It was nothing but torture. I had to report her to head office in the end. At first, they laughed off my complaint, insinuated I should grow a pair, if you like. But the whole incident had a damaging effect on my working life, to the point, all I wanted to do was stay at home and not bother coming in here. That's never happened to me before, ever. It's a daunting experience, I can tell you. In the end, it was Tracie, my fiancée, who came in here and gave Laura a piece of her mind."

"Oh, do tell us more about that, sir."

"I had to take a sick day, my nerves were shattered by then. Tracie marched in here and pinned her against the wall, so the other members of staff said. A couple of the girls had to intervene and pull her off Laura. Of course, everyone soon realised what was going on, and they stuck by me. They gave Laura the cold shoulder until she was fired by head office."

"How did that come about if your head office didn't believe you in the beginning?"

"A couple of the longer serving members of staff rang the human resources manager and told her what was going on in this branch. They gave an ultimatum, either Laura left or they did. Because the two women had fifty-odd years between them under their belts, HR had to take things seriously. I was initially let down by them, but they came good in the end, and Laura was escorted off the premises on the Friday of that week. In truth, it's taken me all this time to get back on track, and now you've come along and forced me to live through that dreadful ordeal again."

"I regret that, Mr Joyston, and I'm so sorry if it's brought back bad memories for you."

"I'll get over it, eventually. Now, if you don't mind, I have another customer to attend to."

"Of course. One last question, if I may?"

"Make it quick."

"Did other male members of staff ever have a problem with her trying to come on to them? Was that ever ascertained during an internal enquiry perhaps?"

"Nothing like that occurred, an enquiry, I mean. Head office just wanted to put the situation to bed, which suited me at the time. With Laura dismissed, I didn't feel the need to involve the staff further, so the subject never arose."

"Would it be possible to speak with the male staff who were employed at the time, sir?"

"There are only two here. I wouldn't have any objections to that, if they're up for it."

"Excellent news."

The three of them left the office together. Mr Joyston took them to the staffroom and asked Sara and Carla to get comfortable while he rounded up the two men.

"I feel sorry for him, don't you?" Carla murmured.

"Definitely. Again, all it's done is highlight how bad Laura is and make me question why we're putting so much effort into finding her. Is it wrong of me to feel this way?"

"Hard to tell. The woman is missing. No one deserves to be abducted, if that's what's going on here. I'm in two minds whether that's true or not now."

"And there we have it. What if she's toying with people and has deliberately run off somewhere? Shit! I can't explain why I have a downer on this one. Oh wait, yes I can, I hate the thought of someone making a fool of us all—you, me, the team and the chief."

Joyston returned with two men, one somewhat taller than him and the other shorter. Sara guessed both men to be in their late twenties.

"These are Greg and Dale. I need to get back to work now. Guys, tell the officers what you told me."

Joyston exited the room, and the four of them sat around the table. Carla took out her notebook.

"Thanks for taking time out to speak with us. I'm presuming Mr Joyston informed you about why we're here? Which of you is Greg?"

"I am," the taller man said.

"Did you have any dealings with Laura Tyler?"

He shook his head slowly. "Not really, nothing like what the boss went through. When that surfaced, we were all appalled beyond words. She seemed nice enough when she first joined us, although she was never what I would class a team player."

Dale nodded. "I would echo that."

"Did you have any dealings with her?"

"Not really. I recall one incident where I found her staring at me while she made Mr Joyston a cup of coffee one day. I was tempted to engage with her in a conversation but went off the idea."

"May I ask why?"

"I suppose I chickened out. I don't have a lot of success with women, you see. Saying that, when the news broke, I heaved out a sigh of relief that I never followed up on my idea."

"I see. Were there any other male members of staff around that time, can you recall?"

The two men consulted each other and then shook their heads. "No. Tony Franks used to work here, but he was long gone before she arrived," Dale said.

"Okay, gents, thanks for speaking to us. I'll give you one of my cards. If anything should come to mind, regarding Laura and her behaviour, will you ring me?"

"Of course. The boss mentioned she's gone missing. Do you know what's happened to her?" Dale asked.

"Not yet, hence our coming here to question your boss. We'll find out, eventually, we always do."

"I hope you find her soon," Dale added.

The two men escorted them back to the entrance.

Sara breathed in a lungful of fresh air as they left the bank. "Again, no further forward."

"I wouldn't necessarily say that. We've added a gem to her character traits. I'd say she can definitely be classed as a maneater now."

"As if there was any real doubt about that. It doesn't excuse why someone would take her, though, if that's what's happened. Come on, let's get back to the station. See what the team have gathered this afternoon. I've had it for the day."

"Are we going to pay the ex-hubby a visit in the morning?"

"Yes, that's the plan. Whether I'll ring him or not to make an appointment, well, I haven't decided on that yet."

The incident room was buzzing when they got back. Even though they'd only been gone a couple of hours, the team had been working flat out in their absence and come up with the goods. Sara did the rounds once she had a coffee in her hands.

"Craig, what did the governor offer you?"

"He started off a little cagey at first, but I soon had him eating out of my hand," the enthusiastic young detective said, beaming.

"I'm eager to hear." Sara motioned with her hand to hurry him up.

"In the end, he informed me that Andy was part of a notorious gang inside. A bad gang they kept a constant eye on."

"Interesting. Did you tell him why you were ringing?"

"Yep, he was flabbergasted that Andy had managed to find a girlfriend so quickly after being released and with his dubious record with the opposite sex, his words, not mine."

"I'm inclined to agree with him. What was Laura thinking? Before you all jump down my throat for voicing that, the more we find out about Laura, the more I dislike her. We learned today she almost cost a decent man his job with her behaviour. Did she see Andy as some sort of challenge? Or an easy target to latch on to because of the rape charge? Her former boss also divulged that he thought she was mentally unstable. He actually put it that he felt she had a screw loose, which amounts to the same thing. Sorry, going off track a tad there, Craig. This gang, did the governor mention if their shenanigans ventured outside the prison, or was it purely internal?"

"That he couldn't tell me. I've got a couple of contacts in the force I need to get in touch with. Hopefully they'll be able to answer that question."

"Brilliant. Get on with that and get back to me."

Sara moved on to Barry who had his hand raised. "Barry? What have you got?"

"I finally heard back about the CCTV. We've got a man in the college car park, tampering with her car at around eight p.m. And no, there's no way to identify him as he was dressed all in black."

"Okay, well, at least that adds to the story of her being abducted rather than running off. Anyone else?"

Marissa nodded. Sara moved around the room to her desk.

"I looked into her bank account. She's overdrawn by three grand, boss. She took out a loan on a credit card for another ten grand on interest free, and this afternoon, someone tried to use her card at Lloyds in Hereford. The transaction was denied because there were insufficient funds in her account."

"Interesting, so where has all her money gone? Do we have a picture of this person?"

"The bank manager is going to get back to me tomorrow with regard to both."

She patted Marissa on the shoulder. "Great work, all of you. Okay, let's throw in the towel for this evening. Have a good one."

After collecting her handbag and jacket from the office, Sara left the incident room with the rest of the team. She decided to think happy thoughts on the way home, during the drive, and ran through the aspects of the wedding they'd already got in place, in readiness for discussing the other preparations which needed to be made with Mark later.

That was until her mobile rang. She answered it without looking at the caller ID, thinking it was probably Mark calling to see how far from home she was. "Hi, I'm on my way."

"You are?" a female voice shrieked in response.

Damn! My ex-mother-in-law. What the hell does she want?

"Charlotte, is that you?"

"You know full well it is, unless you've taken my number out of your phone."

"I haven't, and in my defence, I'm driving so I didn't get a chance to look at the caller ID. What can I do for you?"

"It's Donald. He's in hospital. I need your help. Come quickly."

8

Sara indicated and stopped the car at the side of the road. She was equidistant between home and the hospital.

"Why? I mean, why is he in hospital, Charlotte?"

"Just come. I'll fill you in when you get here. It's serious."

"What? Okay, I'll be there. Are you at Hereford hospital?"

"Yes, of course. Hurry."

With that, Charlotte, her overbearing and often impatient ex-mother-in-law, hung up.

Sara spun the car around and switched on the siren. She'd ring Mark once she was there. During the rapid drive back into town, she wondered, more than once, if she was doing the right thing attending just because Charlotte had summoned her.

Bloody hell. What am I getting myself into? I told them both a few months ago to leave me alone, and now this. What if he is actually seriously ill as she suggested? How am I going to handle that after the way they both spoke to me?

"You're going to have to summon up the compassion you once had for them both and go with the flow." She heaved out a shuddering breath. "Not exactly how I planned on ending a busy day."

She parked the car and took a moment to inform Mark. "Hi, are you at home?"

"Nearly. I stopped off and bought a nice piece of steak, thought it would go well with that bottle of red we bought last week and haven't got around to opening yet."

"Sorry, I have an emergency. I'm not sure how long I'm going to be, love. You go ahead. I'll have a jacket spud or something when I get home, how's that?"

"Nonsense. This can wait until tomorrow. Are you allowed to tell me what the emergency is?"

She hesitated for longer than she should have, then announced, "I got a call from Charlotte. She asked me to come to the hospital because Donald has been in some kind of accident. That's all the details I have right now."

"Oh right. Do you think that's wise?"

"I know what you're thinking. After the way they both spoke to me…the trouble is, I wouldn't be me if I didn't show up in their hour of need, would I?"

"No, I suppose you're right. You need to do what's right for you, Sara."

"Thanks for understanding, not that I doubted you wouldn't because you're a kind and considerate individual, and that's why I love you more with each passing day."

"Get away with you. You go, ring me when you can."

"Of course. I'm going in now. I love you."

"Love you more. Don't take any shit from Charlotte."

"I won't. Any sign of trouble and I'll leave, I promise you."

"Good. Take care."

She sprinted into the Accident and Emergency entrance and straight up to the young man sitting behind the reception desk. "Hi, I received a call to say my brother-in-law had been brought in, Donald Ramsey."

"Just a second…yes, they're treating him now. His parents are in the family room." He pointed down the hallway. "Second door on the left."

"Thanks. I'll check in with them." Sara smiled and turned down the corridor. Her heart was beating so loudly it appeared to drown out her footsteps on the tiled floor. She swallowed down the saliva filling her mouth and walked into the room to find Charlotte sobbing in the arms of her husband, Jonathon.

He smiled at her. "There, there, sweetheart. Hey, look who's arrived."

Charlotte's head rose slowly, and she spun around to face Sara. "You came, I didn't think you would."

Sara took a few steps towards the couple. "Of course I came. Have you heard anything?"

"No, they won't tell us how he is. Maybe you could use your influence to find out for us?" Charlotte replied, hope rising in her voice.

"Not sure I've got any influence to use around here but I'll give it my best shot." She exited the room. Being in the same room as Charlotte for a few seconds had a detrimental effect on her breathing. She sucked in a few steadying breaths on her way back to the reception desk. "Hi, sorry to trouble you again. The family are anxious for some kind of word, and I was wondering if the doctor in charge could spare me a few moments."

The young man shook his head. "Sorry, that's not how it works in this department. I don't know how bad your relative is but I can assure you, the doctor would be in there doing his best. He'll inform the family, as and when he has the time to do so. Patience really is the key in this unit."

"I understand. It was worth a try. I'm a police inspector. The family thought I'd be able to use my job to get a speedier update for them. Thanks anyway."

The young guy smiled and winked. "I'll do what I can for you. Let the doctor know the situation. I can't promise anything, though."

"Thank you, that's kind of you."

Before she headed back to the room, the need for a cup of coffee reared its head. She glanced around for a vending machine. There wasn't one in sight.

"There's a coffee machine in the small shop over there," the receptionist said, accurately reading her mind.

"You're a star. Thank you again."

After buying three cups of coffee and collecting half a dozen sachets of sugar and a couple of stirrers, she returned to the family room. Donald's parents were entwined again but flew apart the second she entered.

"Well? What did the doctor say?" Charlotte demanded.

She offered them a paper cup each. Jonathon took his, but Charlotte made no attempt to take hers, so her husband relieved her of it instead.

"I spoke to the guy on reception. He told me it would be a case of waiting it out, to be patient and the doctor will be with us as soon as he's able to. Maybe you can tell me what happened? Is he really bad? That might give us an indication of how long he's likely to be."

Jonathon nodded, removed the lid from his coffee and stirred in a couple of sachets of sugar. "His car is a write-off. The fire brigade had to cut him out of the wreckage."

"Oh my. Where was he?"

"On the dual carriageway between Hereford and Ross. He drove into a lorry coming in the opposite direction, apparently."

"His fault or that of the other driver?" she asked, slipping into detective mode.

"Does it matter?" Charlotte snapped.

Sara stared at her for a moment or two. In the end, she chose to ignore Charlotte's outburst and sipped at her sweet coffee. The room fell silent; a strained atmosphere had descended. Not pleasant at all, and if Sara had the option to be anywhere else right then, she would've jumped at it.

Bless him, Jonathon, who had always had a soft spot for Sara, or so she thought, must have realised how uncomfortable she felt and did his best to strike up a conversation with her. "How's work?"

Sara swept her fringe back with her left hand. "Busier than ever and—"

Charlotte gasped and pointed at Sara's hand. "My God! You're *engaged*."

Sara closed her eyes. *Shit! Why didn't I bloody take my ring off? I'm not ready to tackle this, not here, not now. Dammit, why should I? I'm engaged to Mark and proud of it.* She nodded. "That's right."

"How long?" Charlotte screeched.

Jonathon placed an arm around his wife's shoulder. "Now, dear, don't go getting yourself upset. Sara is entitled to live her life as she sees fit. Philip left us more than three years ago now."

Sara smiled. "Thank you, Jonathon. I appreciate your understanding."

"I don't," Charlotte yelled. "How could you?"

"Quite easily. I fell in love with a wonderful man. We intend sealing our love with a wedding that I should be at home planning now, except I had no hesitation in responding to your plea to be here."

Charlotte's eyes narrowed. She took a step towards Sara. Suddenly her hand connected with Sara's face. Sara stared down at the coffee she spilt rather than look at Charlotte. Jonathon intervened. He hurriedly placed his cup down on one of the chairs and grabbed his wife by the shoulders.

He turned her to face him. "What in God's name are you doing, woman? How dare you treat Sara like that, how bloody dare you? After all she's done for you and been to this family over the years."

Charlotte had the decency to drop her head, shame clearly enveloping her. She muttered, "I'm sorry. I don't know what came over me."

Sara placed a hand over her flaming cheek. The slap had stung her, and her skin was still bristling with pain. "Charlotte, I have to say this. Philip will always be a huge part of my life; I loved the very bones of that man until the day he died. His death knocked the stuffing out of me. I truly never dreamed I would ever find another man capable of bestowing as much love as Philip gave me, but I was wrong. Mark is everything Philip ever was. He's caring, compassionate to a fault. I would be foolish to give up on love at my young age. It took me a while to fall for Mark. Philip's memory pushed away any thought of happiness, but I overcame that when Mark saved my cat's life. The cat Philip bought me before he died. Rightly or wrongly, I took that as a sign that Philip was watching over me and that he was pushing us together."

Charlotte appeared stunned by her admission. "I see. How exactly did this Mark save your cat's life?"

"He's a vet. Misty was poisoned. It was touch and go whether she lived or not; he saved her."

"Poisoned? Intentionally?" Jonathon asked.

"Yes." She inhaled a breath then let it seep out slowly. "There's something else I haven't told you."

"Go on, surprise us. You're not pregnant, are you?" Charlotte barked.

"Charlotte!" Jonathon reprimanded swiftly.

"No. Okay, I'll leave things there. You're obviously not prepared to listen to anything I have to say. Judging me won't help, Charlotte. I'm young, I have every right to live my life how I see fit, with or without your damned consent. I don't need that, I never have, although that seems to be something you're keen to forget."

"Sara, please, don't do this, not now," Jonathon pleaded, tears welling up in his grey eyes.

"I'm sorry. That was uncalled for. I shouldn't have mentioned Misty being poisoned."

"But you did. So come on, let's hear what you have to say," Charlotte urged, seemingly annoyed.

Sara sank into the chair behind her and encouraged Jonathon and Charlotte to do the same. Jonathon pulled on his wife's arm, and they sat opposite her.

"Last year, the gang who killed Philip targeted me and my home."

Charlotte gasped and reached for her husband's hand.

"Go on," Jonathon said.

"Lots of things happened. A broken window, graffiti left on my front door, that sort of thing. It all escalated when Misty got poisoned. As I said, Mark saved her. The gang members must have been watching the house. They kidnapped Mark and held him hostage. Ended up using him as a bargaining tool."

"For what?" Jonathon asked, perplexed.

"We had to do a swap, the gang leader for Mark."

"What?" Charlotte's mouth dropped open.

"It was a well-constructed plan. I worked with DI Smart in Liverpool."

"But he told us the gang leader had tried to escape."

"He might have fabricated the truth at the time; we made that decision together."

"Oh my. Your friend, was he hurt?" Charlotte asked, surprising Sara.

"He was roughed up a little. Nothing too bad. It did put a slight strain on our relationship at the time, but we came through it, nevertheless."

"I'm glad," Charlotte mumbled. Her chin dipped. "I'm sorry for overreacting, Sara."

"It's okay. I totally understand. If it'll make you feel any better, I still have Philip's last message to me stored on my phone, and I listen to it most days."

"You do? How wonderful."

The door opened, and a youngish male doctor with a few days of stubble walked in. "I can't be long. I understand you want an update on Donald. Well, it would appear he has internal bleeding that needs to be addressed urgently, therefore I've arranged for him to go down for an emergency operation. That will happen within the next fifteen minutes." The doctor raised a hand, warding off any questions the three of them might wish to ask. "His other injuries include two broken legs, a broken arm, four broken ribs and a bad knock to the head which we'll be assessing using an MRI scan. But, saying all that, I do believe he's a fighter and will pull through this. I don't have time to answer your questions, I want to continue monitoring his vital signs until he goes down for surgery."

He smiled and left the room.

Charlotte's head collapsed against her husband's chest. "Oh no, what will I do if I lose Donald as well?"

"Hush now. You heard what the doctor called him, a fighter. He'll pull through this, love. You need to try and remain positive." He rolled his eyes up to the ceiling and gave Sara a weak smile.

"But there's every chance he won't make it if they can't stop the internal bleeding, isn't there?" Charlotte sobbed, her shoulders quivering.

"Please, don't think about that. He's strong, his body will cope with the trauma, I'm sure it will," Sara tried her best to reassure the couple.

The room fell silent, everyone lost in their own thoughts for the next ten minutes until the doctor entered the room again.

"Donald is on his way to surgery. I'm happy with how he's progressing, however, a word of caution: he's not out of the woods yet and not likely to be for a few days minimum. Please bear that in mind."

"Thank you, Doctor. Perhaps you can tell us how long the surgery is likely to take and when we'll be able to see him?" Sara asked.

"The surgery could take anything from a couple of hours up to six or seven. That can't be determined until the surgeon opens him up to see the extent of the damage. As to the other part of your question, I would suggest you all go home and come back tomorrow, however, I'm aware that's asking the impossible of you. He's a close family member, and of course you'd want to be here when he wakes up. In truth, we haven't got an inkling when that's likely to be right now."

Charlotte and Jonathon both shook their heads.

"We're here for the duration," Jonathon stated adamantly.

"Very well. I must get on, it's always a busy time around here." He smiled and left the room.

"Thank you, Doctor," Sara managed to get out before the door shut behind him. "Take heart from what the doctor said, both of you. I'm sorry to say this, but I have to leave now. I'm involved in an important case, and there's no way I can hang around here until Donald wakes up."

"You're *leaving us*?" Charlotte whispered, tweaking Sara's guilty gene.

"Yes. You can ring me later, if you would? I'd like to know how he gets on with his operation."

"If you cared, you'd stay here with us," Charlotte added unnecessarily.

Sara glanced over at Jonathon for help.

He nodded and motioned for her to go. "Go on, lass, thank you for coming. We'll give you a call the minute we hear anything."

Relief overwhelmed her. She got the impression that if Charlotte had been there alone, she would have expected Sara to bed down for the night there and hold her hand. "Thanks, I'd like to know. I'll drop back after work tomorrow, if that's all right?"

"If that's what you want, Sara. We'll leave the decision up to you."

"I promise, workload permitting, that I'll be here tomorrow. Take care, both of you." She crossed the room and pecked each of them on the cheek.

"Goodbye, dear. We appreciate you coming," Jonathon said. He squeezed his wife's shoulder as if urging her to say something.

"Yes, thank you for coming. We'll see you soon, Sara."

She left the hospital and rang Mark's mobile. "I'm leaving now."

"Is everything all right?"

"I'll tell you all about it when I get home."

"Drive carefully. See you soon."

She ended the call and turned up the compilation CD she was listening to when Aretha Franklyn and George Michael's classic song came on. The journey home was carried out on autopilot.

Mark opened the door to greet her with a much-needed kiss. "You look done in. How did it go?"

"I am. I could do with a glass of wine or something stronger. I'll get changed first and fill you in after, if that's all right?"

"Of course it is. On you go."

She wearily made her way upstairs and changed into her cat-style onesie. Mark ordered her to take a seat in the lounge. There was a glass of red wine waiting for her. He entered the room with a tray containing her evening meal.

"Oh, Mark, you didn't have to go to this much trouble."

Steak, mushrooms, tomatoes and a small jacket potato stared up at her.

"It was no bother, I promise."

Between mouthfuls, she revealed the truth about Donald's condition.

"Bloody hell. That's some list of injuries the guy has to deal with. Let's hope he's a good healer and strong enough to withstand the trauma. Internal bleeding would be my main concern."

"I know. I feel for Charlotte and Jonathon."

"How were they holding up when you left them?"

"Okay, I suppose. Umm…we had a little contretemps before the doctor told us about Donald's injuries." She faced him, winced and chewed her lip.

He took the empty tray from her and placed it on the coffee table. "About what?"

Sara held her left hand up and pointed to her engagement ring. "This."

"Heck…what, they told you off for getting engaged?"

"Yeah. Charlotte had a pop. Jonathon did his best to defuse the situation before it got out of hand. I felt very uncomfortable about it all the same."

"As in, you've got regrets?"

She placed a hand to his cheek. "No, I'd never have regrets. No, that's not true, I regret them finding out the way they did. I guess I should have felt obligated to have told them the news first-hand."

"What's done is done. I'm sorry you've had to deal with the added stress on top of everything else. How was work?"

"A pain in the rear." She then spent the next ten minutes going over the Laura Tyler case.

"Jesus, so what's your next move?"

She leaned her head back against the couch. "I wish I knew the answer to that. I still have the ex-husband to speak with yet, maybe he'll be able to give us a clue. If not, then we're going to have to look deeper into everyone's background and shake a few trees to see what comes loose."

"But you're thinking this has something to do with the boyfriend and his cronies in prison, yes?"

"It's the best we can do right now."

He grinned and kissed her. "I bet you're more ticked off that you're on the hunt for clues for a dubious character, knowing you."

"You've nailed it. If it wasn't for the chief asking me to do her a favour, I believe I probably would've given up on Laura Tyler by now."

"I wouldn't blame you in the slightest, but I don't suppose the woman has done that much wrong, not to warrant someone going to the extremes of abducting her anyway."

"Yeah, and that's what's bugging me the most. No matter what my feelings are towards the woman, from the details I've heard so far, she didn't deserve to be kidnapped. Lord knows where she's being kept and what's happening to her. She's been gone around forty-eight hours now."

"Let's try not to dwell on it, you need your rest. Want to watch a movie?"

"Put on something you want to watch, I don't think I'll be able to keep my eyes open much longer. Oh, shit! We're supposed to be making plans for the wedding tonight."

"It'll keep. There's no rush. We'll do it at the weekend when we've got more time, all right?"

"What did I ever do to deserve a man like you?"

"You were lucky to find me single at the time, that's for sure."

They laughed and snuggled up together on the couch. Mark selected a film on Netflix which they'd put aside for a while. Sara saw the opening ten minutes and dropped off to sleep. She woke up a couple of hours later as the end credits were going up.

She stretched. "Blimey, I needed that. I hope I bloody sleep when I go to bed."

"You will. Why don't you go up? I'll see to Misty's needs and be with you soon."

"Where is she? I haven't seen her since I got home."

"Last time I saw her she was curled up on the chair in the kitchen. Go on, up you go."

She fell into bed, played Philip's final message to her, as usual, and dropped off to sleep.

9

Laura shivered. The cold filling the barn had seeped into her bones a long time before. She had no form of blanket at her disposal. The man hadn't returned all day, not since he'd thrown her food on the floor. She'd struggled against her restraints to reach an insignificant amount of the slop on offer. The morsel she had managed to reach contained grime and dirt from the floor which caused her to heave. It was the lack of water in the time she'd been held captive that concerned her the most. Small cracks had already developed on her lips.

She craned her neck to listen, hoping the man would return. All she heard were the sounds of the night. A dog barking in the distance gave her a sense of comfort that she was close to civilisation still. Tears bulged and escaped, dripping onto her cheek. Normally, she'd have the strength to wipe them away. Right now, she neither had the strength nor the willingness to clean herself up. What was the point?

Regrets swam into her mind. *Is this what karma looks like? Has she visited and taken her revenge on my soul? Why? Who would do this to me? I haven't been that bad over the years, have I?*

She shuddered as an owl hooted overhead, nesting in the crossbeam above her. Would she ever get used to the noises going on around her without freaking out? *What am I saying? Why would I want to get used to them? Hopefully, I won't have to stay here much longer. It's all I have to cling on to. The hope that someone will find me or that the man will let me go after a few days. Hope is all I've got at the end of the day. I'll cling on to that tightly...for as long as I'm able to, but without proper food and water, how long is that likely to be?*

Another noise caught her attention. She sucked in a breath. Yes, it was a car. *It's him, he's coming back. Why? What are his plans?* A car door...the padlock being unlocked...her heart rate doubled within a few tension-filled seconds.

The man's silhouette filled the doorway with the moon lighting up the night sky behind him. She froze, uncertain whether to speak or to ignore him. Decisions were hard to come by when faced with such adversity—it hadn't taken long for that to dawn on her.

He approached her, his steps slow and deliberate. Her gaze dropped to the carrier bag in his right hand. *Is that food? Water? Please, let it be one or the other.*

"Enjoying the facilities, are you?"

She stared up at him. She didn't recognise him at all. The fact that he was showing her his face confused her. What did that mean? *That when this, whatever this is, when it's all over he's going to do away with me? Doesn't he care that I might be able to identify him to the police, if I survive this ordeal?*

His hand dipped into the bag. He placed a plastic bottle of water at his feet, followed by what appeared to be, and smelt like, a drive-through meal. Again, the items were placed out of reach. She didn't know whether to plead to have them or ignore them altogether. Her mind was all over the place, due to dehydration and lack of nourishment.

The man turned to walk away. She automatically reached for the food and drink—her fingertips were over six inches from both. Tears of frustration sprang to her eyes and blurred her vision.

"Please, please, don't do this. I need water. I need food. Don't torture me this way."

His evil laughter echoed around the barn, and he paused, glared at her, and then slammed the door shut again.

"Please," she shouted, the single word ripping her throat raw.

The car engine started, and she listened to it trundle back down the track. She was alone again, alone and scared, with the temptation to satisfy her cravings within spitting distance of her.

What have I done to deserve this?

Am I going to die here?

With no food or drink, surely that's what will happen.

The chain bit into her ribs. She didn't remember them being that prominent before. Would that have happened within forty-eight hours? She doubted it. Probably her mind playing tricks on her. She tried every which way possible to reach at least one of the items and failed each time.

Why? Someone must really hate me to do something this sadistic.

~

He rang his contact. "Yep, food and water delivered, placed three feet away from her as requested."

"Good. How's she coping?"

"I'd say she isn't. She pleaded for me not to go. I laughed and bolted from the barn. How long to go now?"

His contact chuckled. "She'll get what's coming to her soon enough. Just keep delivering the food. The smell and sight of it sitting there will be enough to drive her crazy in the end. We need to up our game in the other department."

"Meaning what?"

A sigh travelled down the line. "The boyfriend. We need to start setting him up."

"Okay. You haven't told me how to do that, you only hinted at it."

"Leave it with me. A plan is brewing. I'll get back to you when I've had a chance to think things through properly. Hang tight until then. I'll put some money in your account this evening."

"Half the money?"

"I'm not that stupid. I'll give you a quarter of what's due and a hundred extra for the food."

"By that I take it you don't trust me."

"I didn't say that. Let's put it this way, I prefer to think of it as keeping you on your toes."

"I won't let you down." He laughed. "I'm enjoying it too much."

"Good. Keep up the good work. I've got to go."

"Ring me tomorrow with further instructions."

"I'll do that."

His contact ended the call. He drove to the nearest pub, downed a pint, and then headed home, thoughts of the girl in the barn pushed to the very back of his mind, for now.

10

"Okay, let's run through what we have on the agenda this morning." Sara addressed the team at a little after nine. "First thing, Carla and I will be going out to see the ex-hubby. Craig, can you chase up what the detectives have to say about the gang members, and what type of crimes they get up to on the outside for me?"

"Already noted down to do ASAP, boss."

"Good. Jill, can you keep digging into Laura's past? Previous jobs and possible boyfriends, just in case we have to go down that route?"

"Leave it with me," Jill replied.

"You'll be chasing up Lloyds about the ATM pictures this morning, right, Marissa?"

She nodded. "Want me to look into Laura's bank details a little deeper, too?"

"Why not? I think we have enough elements to be going on with, it's a case of scratching deeper to see what we can find."

Sara studied the board with all the names on it. "One of these people knows something more than they're letting on, that's my hunch. Actually, it's more than a hunch. Our main suspect at this point has to be Andy. Let's not lose sight of that but also keep an open mind about all the others up here. Okay? We'll grab a quick coffee, Carla, before we head off. There's no telling when we'll likely get another one, and I'm not ready to function properly without that extra dose of caffeine in my veins. I'll be going through my post, if you could bring it in for me?"

Carla tutted. "If I have to."

Sara grinned and entered her office which was bathed in sunshine. She sat behind her desk, picked up the phone and rang the hospital.

The news was better than she had anticipated. Donald had come through his surgery without any hitches but up until then was still unconscious. Sara asked the nurse to pass on her best wishes to his parents and hung up.

"Someone in hospital?" Carla asked, coming in on the tail end of the conversation.

"Yep. Philip's brother. He's in a bad way. Multiple fractures and a few broken ribs plus internal bleeding which they think they've sorted out."

"Shit! What happened?"

"His car had an argument with a lorry. The vehicle's a write-off."

Carla whistled. "I'm not surprised. I'm amazed he got out of it alive if his car was crunched to that degree."

"Yeah, I suppose you're right."

"You had a really long day yesterday then?"

"I did. I'm hoping for an easier one today. I doubt that's going to be the case, though. I'm looking forward to seeing what Laura's ex has to say about her, aren't you?"

"Sort of. Experience tells me it isn't going to be pleasant, which is why he's an ex."

Sara sipped her drink and nodded. "Yep, I predict you're right. Thankfully, there's not a lot of post to go through. I'll be out in a few minutes, maybe ten tops."

"In other words, go and make yourself useful elsewhere, right?"

Sara grinned at Carla. "Glad we're on the same wavelength."

She tackled the post which included a few minor changes in procedure, some of which would benefit her team in the future. She'd apprise them of the changes once the case was over. There was no need to rush things through yet.

After finishing her drink, she collected Carla, and they left the building. The drive out to Bobby Tyler's address took them through the town and out into the countryside to Tillington Common. His home was one of the newer houses in the pretty village. It consisted of a timber frame which was dominated by glass on the front elevation.

"Wow, this is something out of one of those self-build magazines," Sara stated and killed the engine.

"I'd love to live in a place like this. I'm betting I'll never get the opportunity, not on a DS's wage."

"Hey, if it's any consolation, I doubt I'm ever going to manage to buy a place like this on my meagre wage either."

"Yeah, but at least you'll be getting married to a vet. His wage is probably three times what my fella earns as a fireman."

"True enough. Let's not compete, hon. It is what it is." She patted her partner on the thigh, and they left the vehicle.

They walked through the large single wooden gate which was open. There was a Mazda MX5, its engine running and the driver's door open, sitting on the drive close to the entrance. A blonde woman, wearing a pink tunic top and pristine white trousers, tore out of the house and almost bumped into Sara.

"Sorry, I wasn't expecting to find someone standing on my doorstep." She eyed them both warily.

Sara produced her ID. "DI Sara Ramsey and DS Carla Jameson. Is Mr Tyler in?"

"Yes. I'll give him a shout for you." She opened the door again which she'd slammed shut a few seconds before and shouted, "Bobby, there's someone at the door to see you."

"Tell them to sod off and come back later, I'm in the bathroom," his reply echoed in the hallway.

"I'll let you into the lounge. You can wait there for him. I'll shoot upstairs and tell him to get a shift on. What's this about?"

"A case we're investigating."

"Oh right. If you're not prepared to tell me, it's okay with me, I'm not hanging around anyway. I only dropped back for my bag. I'm late for work, so if you'll excuse me."

"That's fine. Thanks for letting us in."

She thundered up the stairs and descended them a little while later and left the house. Sara had a brief nose around the living room, at the photos of an older man with the young woman who had let them in. The room was large and filled with obscurely shaped ornaments in silver and bronze, some of which Sara presumed could be used as vases. She crossed the room to the patio doors and glanced out at the immaculate garden. "Bloody hell, there's a huge pool out here as well. It's all right for some."

"Hard work has paid off in my case," a male voice responded.

Sara's cheeks flared up, and she spun around. "Sorry, I didn't hear you come down."

"I don't tend to stomp around the house like my wife does. She told me who you are, what she didn't tell me was why you're here."

Sara held her hand out to shake his and showed him her warrant card. "DI Sara Ramsey. It's a general enquiry really, if you can spare us ten minutes of your time?"

"Please, take a seat. You're lucky to catch me in. I decided to work from home today as I have a lot of conference calls to make with clients abroad. Sometimes it's easier to do them here than at work. There's a lot of construction going on opposite us, and you never know when a pneumatic drill is going to start up."

Sara and Carla sat together on one of the cream couches, and he sat in a black leather swivel chair.

"Makes sense. What business are you in, Mr Tyler?"

"My company exports medical equipment around the world."

"I see. How long have you been running your business?"

"This particular one around ten years. I've had several throughout my working life, some more prosperous than others. This one happens to be my most successful to date."

"I'm pleased it's all working out for you. Do you get to travel much?" she asked, intrigued to find out more about his business in case he was behind Laura's disappearance. Images of overseas containers flooded into her mind and Laura being kept in one, ready to be shipped out to distant shores.

"I wish. Only on holidays. Back in the day, before the internet came along, yes, there was a vast amount of travel involved in my work, sadly not much now. Although, sometimes I wished there was."

Sara tilted her head. "Care to elucidate on that?"

He chewed on his lip, giving her the impression that he'd spoken out of turn. "You've seen my wife. Let's just say she can be a tad overpowering at times, and the idea of having a break for a few days can be very appealing."

"Ah, I'm with you. Have you been married long? Sorry, I didn't catch your wife's name."

"It's Gillian." He let out a long sigh and added, "Three years. I think I married on the rebound but I'd never utter those words to her, of course."

"On the rebound?"

"Yes, my first marriage ended a few months before I met her. I was out drowning my sorrows one day at a pub, bumped into Gillian and, well…I don't suppose I need to fill in the rest of the details for you."

"No, I think I can manage to work out the specifics myself. But you love her, right?"

"Of course I do. I wasn't saying that. Oh bugger, ignore me. I think we should move on, don't you?"

"If you insist. Talking of your first wife, can you tell me if you've seen Laura lately?"

"Not for a few months. I spotted her across the road from me in town, called over to her, but she chose to ignore me. That kind of sliced me in two at the time."

"It did? May I ask why?" Sara asked. Again, her interest rose a few notches.

"Up until that time, our split had been quite amicable. It puzzled me why she would react like that."

"Did you manage to speak and have it out with her?"

"No. I was running late for a meeting and couldn't spare the time, otherwise I would have."

"Did you try and call her?"

"No. I left well alone. I appreciated I was being foolish. Laura made her decision to cut me out of her life. I realised after our marriage ended that you can't force someone to speak to you if they really don't want, or can't be bothered, to hold a conversation with you."

"I suppose that's true."

"Why are you asking me these questions, Inspector?"

"Well, on Tuesday of this week, Laura went missing."

"Missing? As in, took off and hasn't been seen since?"

"That's right. Would you happen to know anything about that, Mr Tyler?"

"Call me Bobby. No, why should I? Unless you're suggesting I had something to do with it?" He pushed himself out of his chair and paced the centre of the room.

"Sit down, sir. That's not what I was getting at."

"Why should I? If you're going to persist in questioning me."

"Please. As I've already stated, we're not here to question you as such, we're hoping you'll help us with our enquiries."

He threw himself back into his chair and swivelled it back and forth. Sara sensed this motion was soon going to get on her nerves.

"What do you need to know? Apart from me not seeing her recently."

"Has she contacted you?"

"No. I've already told you that."

"Okay, please, try and remain calm, getting irate isn't going to help either of us, is it?"

"I don't know, it's a defence mechanism for me, if I'm being accused of doing something to an ex, not that I've ever been in this position before. Where did she go missing?"

"Close to her work."

He shrugged. "That's not helpful, I don't know where she worked. The last I heard she'd left NatWest bank. That was her last known role."

"Yes, she left there under a cloud. We've already spoken to her former boss."

"Are you telling me she stole from the bank?"

"No, not at all. I can't tell you what the circumstances were for her dismissal."

"Then what?"

"We're trying to ascertain details of Laura's past. That's where you come in."

"What about her past?"

"When you were married to her, did she keep any secrets from you perhaps?"

"Secrets? That seems a daft question. Think about it, how would I know if they were secrets?"

"Okay, let me rephrase my question, make it much clearer for you. Maybe you can tell us why your marriage broke up?"

He fell silent for a few seconds. He focussed on his hands wringing together for a second or two and then glanced up at Sara again. "Yes, she lied to me. We were trying for a baby, and she lied, told me she was pregnant. After six months of not developing a bump"—he raised a hand to stop Sara from interrupting him, then continued—"she went to the loo one day and announced she'd just flushed the baby down the toilet."

"Flushed it down the toilet? You mean she had a miscarriage and lost it?"

"Yes. However, those were her exact words."

"Was she upset or traumatised by the event?"

"No. I was, but she simply went with the flow. That's what made me suspect she was lying to me. I did some digging with the hospital—she had never registered with them for the scans she'd told me she'd attended. God, she even showed me a picture of a foetus, its cute little arms and legs on show. I fell for it, hook, line and sinker. More fool me, right?"

"Did she say why?"

"She told me she was jealous of it. Not that there ever was one. She admitted she wanted to see how I would react to her if ever she informed me that we were expecting a child."

"And how did you react, Bobby?"

"Looking back, I suppose I'm guilty of overreacting. I treated her well, gave her everything she needed. Even told her to give up work, which she did. To have her lie about something so important, well...it fucking crucified me, I can tell you."

"I'm sorry to hear that. Were there any other moments similar to that during your marriage?"

"I don't honestly know. I think she might have made up stuff about her father somewhere along the line."

Sara and Carla exchanged a quick glance. "Can you tell me what that entailed?" Sara asked.

He stared at a patch of the multi-coloured rug in front of him. "I don't know whether I should say or not, I doubt if it was the truth, knowing how she lied about the baby."

"Can you tell us?"

"Her version is that her father abused her as a child."

"Ouch! Okay, did she say if that was in the form of mental or physical abuse and if the authorities were involved?"

"Physical, and I believe that's why her parents split up. What I had trouble figuring out is why she kept in contact with her father. Would you? I know I wouldn't."

"No, I don't think I would've been able to do that. But it takes all sorts to make this world, as we're finding out daily."

"I just found it odd."

"Did you tackle her about her reasoning behind her decision?"

"She refused to tell me. I can tell you it put a strain on our relationship in more ways than one."

"Can you clarify that?"

"In the bedroom department and life in general, I suppose."

"I understand, it must've been hard for you?"

"It was, exceptionally hard. Everyone hopes their first marriage will be a success. I think we tend to go out of our way and try harder, don't we? Well, I never got the feeling that she was either willing, or capable, of making it a success."

"Sorry to hear that. So, was it you who initiated the divorce proceedings?"

He shook his head, and a sadness etched into his features. "Not in the slightest, that was down to her. I pleaded with her to see a therapist or to go to counselling with me, but she refused to do it."

"Did she give you a reason for her reluctance?"

"No, not really. Just said it wasn't her and that she abhorred that type of thing. Maybe a specialist would have been able to see right through her. Oh, I don't know. The more I suggested it, the more she got pissed off with me. Come the end, I stopped talking about it. Our marriage declined into a farce, and she sat me down one day and told me she wanted out."

"How did you respond?"

"I was devastated. I had to accept it, what else could I do? She moved out, we sold our fantastic house, and I gave her half of the proceeds. I moved in here soon after, and that's when I met Gillian."

"I'm glad you've met someone else. I take it Gillian has been a huge support to you?"

"She has. I'm not sure what I was thinking marrying Laura. She and Gillian are total opposites. I'll correct that, maybe not totally, but they are definitely vastly different."

"I take it she's some kind of hairdresser perhaps, judging by her uniform?" Sara knew what his wife's role was; this was her way of covering up that they'd delved into his background. There was no need to hint at that.

"Almost. She's a beautician, owns her own salon, which is a phenomenal success. It was a thriving business long before I came along. She's self-sufficient, never asks me for money, ever."

"Good to know you both have enterprising companies to your names. Getting back to Laura. During your marriage, was there anything else which happened that raised your suspicions?"

"In what respect?"

"Did Laura ever mention having problems with someone at work or something along those lines?"

He paused to think. "I don't recall that being the case. Maybe I'm just not thinking straight right now. I can't believe she's gone missing.

Are you telling me you think something sinister has happened to her?"

"Truthfully, we're not sure, and that's why we're visiting everyone she knows. My belief is that something in her past is behind her disappearance. The question is, what?"

"I can't help you, apart from what I've already told you. Maybe it would be worth you contacting her father, to see if she was telling the truth there."

"We've been in touch. He didn't mention the abuse, not that I think he would during a general enquiry call. We'll do some digging, see if anything shows up in our records."

"What about her best friend, Cas? They were always on the phone to each other, several times a day. Used to drive me loopy when I was with her."

"We've spoken to Cas. Apparently, they fell out a few months ago."

"Never! Did she say why?"

"Man trouble, as in, Cas found Laura in bed with Cas's boyfriend one day."

"Whoa! That's unbelievable." He shook his head, his eyes open as wide as saucers.

"It's the truth. Well, if there's nothing else you can tell us, we'll be on our way."

"I've racked my brain to try and help you. Maybe if you leave a card and something comes to mind, I can call you."

Sara stood and handed him a card.

He saw them back through the house. "I hope she turns up soon. I hate to think of her out there all alone."

"We hope so, too. Thanks for agreeing to speak to us. Sorry if we've caused you to be late for any of your calls."

"You haven't." He waved them off and closed the door as they neared the gate.

Sara pulled it to behind her, and they got in the car.

"What's your immediate thoughts about him?" Carla asked before Sara had the chance to voice the same question.

"He comes across as believable, genuine even. Nice snippet he dropped in there about Laura's father. We need to see if there's anything on file about that when we return to base."

"Again, the jury is still out for me. Why fake a pregnancy like that? Who does that?"

"A desperate woman trying to hang on to her man. That's my best guess, anyway. For something that should have been a cut-and-dried case, this is turning out to be anything but. If only we could trace her phone, I think that would hold the key."

"We could get a log for her calls, that might help us," Carla suggested.

"Maybe. I mean yes, of course it will. Let's get the ball rolling on that as soon as we get back. I think we've exhausted all of our options out in the field now. It's back to the station to begin dig, dig, digging into everyone we've come into contact with so far. At the end of the day, it's all we've got going for us, right?"

"Well, you're not wrong, as frustrating as that might be."

11

Calum Richardson received a text from his contact instructing him what to do next. He was on his way back to the barn.

He arrived and took his bag of goodies with him. After he'd unlocked the barn, he stared at the woman. All feelings for her dead to him. If the choice was his, he'd let her perish here. But his contact didn't want that…not yet.

It was too soon. His contact wanted the bitch to suffer, hence the torture technique with the food.

Another drive-through meal was placed on the floor next to another bottle of water. The woman's head lolled to the side—she was sitting upright, no doubt the chunkiness of the chain doing its job in preventing her from lying down on the straw bale.

"You came back," she whispered. "Please, I need water." Her hand reached out, but her arm was far too weak to support it.

"I'll put it here. All you have to do is try and find the strength to seek it out." He laughed, withdrew a pair of scissors from his pocket and took a few steps, invading her personal space. He didn't care about that. He held up a chunk of her hair and snipped it off.

She moved her head from side to side to try to disrupt his plan. In the end, she failed.

He tucked the hair into a plastic food bag and then grabbed her shoulder with one hand, keeping her still while he cut away a piece of her blouse. He stepped away and stared down at her. She repulsed him. All the men she had been with over the years must have needed their heads read. She was filth and now she was sitting in her own mess. It was as if he'd only just noticed the smell of the bodily fluids she had excreted. He kicked her in the leg.

She squealed. Her throat raspy, she pleaded, "Please, don't hurt me. Won't you let me go? You've punished me enough now. Whatever I've done to you in the past, nothing is worth this."

"Isn't it? You really have no dignity at all, do you? Your type never do. You mess with people's lives, not caring about the damage you cause. It's all about you, nothing else matters in this life, except for you."

She shook her head slowly. "I don't understand. Do I know you? I don't remember you."

"Does it matter who I am? No, it doesn't. I'm here with you. Holding you captive, ensuring you realise your mistakes in this world, and boy, there have been many of those over the years, haven't there? Maybe you should use this time to reflect on those."

"I have been. I'm sorry, sorry for everything I've ever done wrong in my life and the people I've hurt."

"Easy for you to say, in your situation. Even then, you're not coming across as believable. I don't hear any kind of remorse in your words. Still…it'll come, providing you can hold on long enough. Do you know how many days a body can keep going without water?"

"No, I must be approaching that. My insides are beginning to hurt, my throat feels cut to ribbons. My voice is faltering. Please, take pity on me and give me some water."

He tipped his head back and laughed again. "No way, José. I'm enjoying this far too much to stop now. I'll be back later. Enjoy your day and keep out of mischief. Don't go doing anything I wouldn't do."

He turned and strode out of the barn, secured it, jumped back in his car and drove away from the site. Halfway down the track, he remembered to send his contact a message.

. . .

All done. I have the evidence. She's beginning to struggle now.

He drove a couple of miles through the country lanes and pulled over to read the response.

Good, I'm thrilled she's suffering. Now carry on, you know what to do next. I'm trusting you to have this in place today.

He typed back:

Don't worry, leave it to me, I've never let you down before.

He waited patiently for a reply, but it never came.

12

Back at the station, Sara called the team together and went through what Bobby had told them. "So, now that Carla and I have questioned all the people on our 'to contact' list, here's what I think we should do next. Feel free to raise any objections along the way." She picked up the marker pen and circled one name. "Andy Palmer. I still maintain he's our main suspect. Does anyone have any reason not to agree with me?" The room remained silent. "Good. Craig and Barry, if you've finished digging into the tasks I set you, I'd like you to begin surveillance on him. When Carla and I questioned him, he didn't seem that perturbed by Laura's disappearance, which bothered me. He seemed far more concerned about the breakfast he'd cooked for himself. Any news from the detectives dealing with the gang, Craig?"

"Sort of. One of them had a recent dealing with a gang member. He's had a few interactions with a couple of them, in fact, over the past couple of months."

"What have they been up to?"

"It's mainly to do with money. One of them was arrested for getting his revenge on a loan shark who'd been screwing his missus while he was banged up, her way of paying off the debt she owed. Another one is suspected of holding up a local post office. They've yet to find the evidence to put him away for that one."

"Interesting. Did you tell the detectives what we're dealing with?"

He nodded. "Yep. The detective said it was unlikely any of the gang would be involved, not unless there was a money aspect to consider."

"Such as a ransom?" Sara asked.

"Exactly. The detective also told me that Palmer had been involved with some minor jobs, screwed up one which earned him a beating."

"Okay, as far as a ransom goes, we haven't had one of those, not yet. Something's telling me we're not going to be getting one either. He sounds as though he's in deep with the gang. Maybe that's an indicator that they could be involved in Laura's disappearance. We'll need to keep a close eye on things. Let's see what he gets up to today, and possibly tomorrow, and go from there. Off you go, keep in touch. If he moves, I want to know ASAP."

"Got that, boss." Craig hitched his jacket on and joined Barry at the door.

Once the men had gone, Sara perched on the nearest desk. "Marissa, any news on the photo from the ATM yet?"

"There is, it came through while you were out. Grainy photo, can't really make out the person. He's wearing a baseball cap and has his collar turned up, at least, I think it's a fella."

She handed the photo to Sara who examined it, angling it in different directions.

"Great. To me, it looks like we're dealing with a professional who is covering their tracks well."

"And to me," Carla said. "Let's hope they slip up."

"It would be nice. I'm conscious of the time which has elapsed since Laura was taken. We still don't know what the motive is behind her going missing. I think we can rule out the most obvious one, for ransom, I don't think her parents are that well off. Had this happened when she was married to Bobby, well, I'm guessing it would've been a different story entirely. Therefore, that leaves the gang scenario. Is Andy still working for them? He's some sort of delivery driver. That leaves the door open with regard to getting about easily enough, doesn't it? Who does he drive for?"

"I couldn't find anything. Want me to see if he's registered with a parole officer?" Jill replied.

"If you would, Jill. Let's focus everything we have on him for now. If we fail to find anything then I haven't got a bloody clue where to go next."

"That's not what I wanted to hear."

Sara shot off the desk and spun around to find DCI Price standing behind her. "Sorry, boss, I didn't see you there."

"That much is apparent. Do you have time for a quick conflab?"

"In my office?"

Carol was already heading that way.

Sara turned to face her partner and cringed. "Can you bring us in a couple of coffees?" She dug into her jacket pocket and pulled out a couple of pound coins.

"Will do. Good luck."

"Thanks. I'll need it by the look of things." She inhaled and exhaled a few steadying breaths and breezed into the office.

Carol was already seated on the visitor's side of the desk. "Thought I'd drop by for an update as you hadn't bothered to come and see me."

"I had every intention of coming to see you during the day. I'm not making excuses, but Carla and I flew out to see the ex-husband this morning. We haven't been back long."

"Excuses or not, I thought we agreed you'd report back to me daily."

She didn't recall promising any such thing. Maybe the chief thought it was expected of her. "Sorry, we've been at it full-on."

"Knock, knock," Carla called out. She set two cups of coffee on the desk and retreated.

"Thanks, Carla. Much appreciated." Sara smiled at her partner and slid one of the cups in front of the chief. "Boss."

"I'll have it in a moment. Well…are you going to tell me what you've found out or not?"

"Not a lot would be the honest answer. Bobby did tell me something that I need to look into today. It's of a sensitive nature."

Carol frowned. "Go on."

"How well do you know the family's background?"

"Give me a hint at what you're getting at?"

"This would've happened when the original family unit was intact."

"You mean when Lin was married to her first husband?"

"That's right. Do you know why they split up?"

"Not really. What have you heard?"

Anxious, Sara ran a hand over her face. "Bobby suggested that Laura's father abused her."

"Holy shit! I've not heard that. I'm not surprised Lin divorced him if that was the case."

"It's something I need to delve into today. To see if there was anything registered with Social Services before I go back to either Lin or Laura's father."

"You've contacted the dad?"

"Yes, he seemed all right over the phone, not that I could really tell, which is why I prefer to see a person face to face."

"Why would Bobby tell you she'd been abused if it wasn't true? What would he have to gain from that?"

Sara shrugged. "I don't know. It's early days yet, we're still digging into people's backgrounds. Maybe it was his way of apportioning the blame for his ex-wife's behaviour during their marriage."

"What else did he say about her?"

"That Laura pretended to be pregnant and had a fake miscarriage."

"Whoa! Why would she do that?"

"Let's just say a lot of negative things have come to light during our investigation."

"Are you going to tell me what they consist of?"

"Cards on the table, I'm getting the impression that Laura isn't a nice person. I know she's a family friend and it's wrong of me to cast aspersions on someone who has disappeared, but the problem is, all that I've heard is hard facts, not mere tittle-tattle by men and women she's scorned, from what I can tell."

"Shit! Okay, that aside for now, do you still think the boyfriend is the main suspect?"

"Yes. I've got a couple of men on surveillance. We'll do that for the next twenty-four to forty-eight hours. Also, her best friend recently dumped her for bedding her boyfriend. Plus, her best friend said she believed Laura was having an affair with her boss. I've yet to tackle him about that. Her boyfriend is an ex-con who appears to be up to his neck in dodgy dealings as a member of a gang of people he hung around with in prison. Can you see where all this is leading?"

"I can. I'm so sorry to have burdened you with this one, Sara."

She waved her boss's concern away. "Don't be. As you can see, nothing is ever easy during an investigation of this magnitude. It doesn't help us knowing all the facts and yet having no actual leads to go on."

"Can you bring the boyfriend in for questioning?"

"We'll keep an eye on him, see what he gets up to for now. One step out of line, and I'll haul his arse into the station and grill him."

"What about the media? Have you actioned an appeal yet?"

"Again, not yet. I wanted to speak with all the friends and exes before I touched on that side of things. It's definitely on my to-do list. It's all so challenging. It would be different if we were dealing with a kidnap and had a ransom to find, but we've got nothing. Is there any way she could have just taken off?"

"I doubt it, she never seemed the type."

"Looking at the missing persons statistics, around ten percent of all those who go missing do so because they don't want to be found. Most of them don't even stick around to pack a bag."

"Oh heck. What are you saying, that you'd rather throw in the towel now?"

"Not at all. I think it's something we should consider, either sooner or later."

"That saddens me. However, maybe you're right. Have you rung Lin?"

"I haven't spoken to her since yesterday. Why?"

Carol reached for her cup and took a sip of her coffee. "Maybe she's had a phone call or text from Laura. Might be worth a call."

"I doubt it. She promised me she'd keep in touch if Laura made contact."

"What do you intend doing about the abuse claims?"

"It's a sticky wicket. I need to do some research first and then decide. It's a tough call. It doesn't detract from what I've been saying all along, though, that Laura is a bit of a maneater. Maybe that issue is the one which eventually came back to haunt her and got her in this mess."

"You're suggesting a man has taken revenge on her?"

"Possibly. I'm probably talking out of my arse. Hell, there's still the fact that Andy is an ex-con who, as far as I know, hasn't been on the straight and narrow since he was released, despite what he told me. How far his dubious ways have led him is anyone's guess right now."

Carol tutted. "I feel guilty for causing you all this trouble."

"You don't have to feel guilty. I feel like I'm letting you down, not having any bloody answers for you."

"It's only been a couple of days, less, just over sixty hours."

"I know. Well, that's you up to date now. I hope you appreciate the frustration running through the team."

"I do. I also have confidence that you'll find Laura, hopefully before anything drastic happens to her."

"That's the aim, although when we'll find her is anyone's guess."

Carol took another sip from her coffee. "Any news on a date for your wedding?"

"Not yet. Mark and I were supposed to sit down and discuss it last night, but by the time I returned from the hospital, it was too late. I fell asleep in the chair."

"Wait, back up. Hospital? Why? It's not your dad, is it?"

"No, Dad's fighting fit, for now. My first husband, not sure what else to call him really, Philip, his brother is in Intensive Care."

"Oh no. Why? What happened to him?"

"His car got mangled by a lorry. Multiple fractures and internal bleeding which they think they've dealt with during emergency surgery. I was with his parents most of the evening, waiting for news."

"Is he going to be all right?"

"I think so. I called the hospital this morning; he's had a comfortable night. I'll drop in on him later, after work."

"Goodness, you do have a lot on your plate."

"It's fine. It seems there's always something personal happening to prevent me from going home and putting my feet up after a busy day at work."

"And then I dump this on you. I appreciate I've put you in an untenable situation. It was selfish of me to ask you to take on this case."

Sara smiled and shook her head. "Stop thinking that, it was nothing of the sort. I'm more annoyed at myself for not finding Laura yesterday. I think you're going to have to prepare yourself for the worst."

"Really? Is that what your gut is telling you?"

"Yes. I sincerely hope I'm wrong, only time will tell."

"You want me to get out of your hair now, don't you?"

Sara smirked. "You read my mind. We need to chase up a few things that are niggling us. I'll contact you later, if that's all right?"

Carol rose from her seat. "Of course. Good luck."

Her boss departed without smiling, her shoulders positioned in her usual determined stance. Sara's heart went out to her. Carol wasn't the type to wear her heart on her sleeve, and she realised how tough this must be for her to have to contend with. That was why Sara would do her best to solve Laura's disappearance, even though her heart wasn't in it.

Craig contacted the incident room via radio a few hours later. "Boss, we're at Sainsbury's, we followed Palmer here. He appears to be waiting for someone. He's twitchy, looking around him. Not sure if he spotted us or not, so we're keeping our distance for now."

"I see. Okay, are you close enough to see what's going on? You know, should he meet up with anyone?"

"I think so, we've got the camera set up, ready to go."

"Keep me informed."

"Wait. Hang on, a car has parked opposite him. A bloke in a hoody is getting out. Andy has exited his vehicle and has gone to the boot. Damn, they're both out of sight now."

There was an anxious wait before Craig spoke again. "Nope, I think it was a false alarm. The newcomer was en route to the supermarket. Andy has remained at the boot; he's looking around him. Seems shifty as fuck…oops, sorry, boss."

Sara chuckled. "I get the message. Is there any way either of you can get close enough to see what's in the boot?"

"Barry said he'll take a wander past him, if that's what you want?"

"Could Palmer have spotted either of you?"

"I don't think so."

"Then let Barry get closer, tell him to…well, I don't need to tell him how to act. Keep the line open, I want to know what's happening as it happens."

"He's on his way now. Hang tight a second, boss."

Sara and the rest of the team all listened in to the radio communication.

After a while, Craig continued his commentary. "Right, Barry has walked past. He's approaching the supermarket entrance and now he's turning back. He should be with me in a few minutes."

"No rush. Is Palmer still in the same position?"

"He is. Hang on…another car has pulled up alongside his…Barry's back now."

"Everything all right, Barry?" Sara asked.

"Yes, boss. He was leaning against the boot, obviously waiting for someone. Looks like that person has arrived. What do you want us to do?"

"Hang fire. Have you got eyes on them?"

"Briefly. If they move another few inches, we're screwed, unless I get out there and find a better position to take photos."

"No, don't risk it. Our intel has told us this is a nasty gang. I don't want you two in the thick of it. If nothing comes from this, then so be it."

"A guy is getting out of the vehicle. He's got a package in his hand and he's approaching Palmer. Interesting…they held the briefest of conversations, and now the guy is returning to his car. He's started the engine and is driving off."

"What's Palmer doing?"

"He's closed down the boot and is now getting back into his vehicle. What do you want us to do?"

"Go. Pick the bastard up now and bring him in. I've got a few things I want to ask him."

"On it. We'll be back soon."

Sara rubbed her hands and nodded at the rest of the team. "The boys have done good. Let's see what the little shit has to say for himself."

13

Sara made her way down to the interview rooms around thirty minutes later. A tsunami of emotions surged through her with every step that took her closer to the suspect. She marched into the room to find Barry and Craig sitting at the table with a shell-shocked Andy on the other side, alongside a female duty solicitor who had been called in.

"We meet again, Mr Palmer."

He glared at her. "What's this all about? You have no right bringing me in here like this. I've done nothing wrong."

"Craig, stay here. Barry, can I see you outside?"

Barry left his chair and followed her out of the room.

"What was in the package?"

"Drugs. Looks like cocaine; it's being tested now. Of course, he denied everything, twat that he is, despite us finding it on his passenger seat."

"Damn idiot. I'll take it from here."

Barry nodded and walked away from her. She prepared herself, fixed a smile in place and entered the room once more. Andy's gaze followed her across to her seat.

THE LIES SHE TOLD

Craig said the necessary blurb to the recording machine and then handed the reins over to Sara.

"Right, Mr Palmer, why don't I call you Andy from here on in?"

"Do what you like. I don't get why you've dragged me in here."

"We've hardly dragged you in. Two members of my team had you under surveillance and saw you pick up a package from a contact. Can you tell us what was in that package?"

His gaze dropped to the table, and he clenched his hands together until his knuckles whitened under the strain. "No comment."

Sara sighed and rolled her eyes. "Really? You want to go down this route?"

"I've advised my client not to say anything further," his solicitor stated.

"Well, we have the package, and it's on the way to the lab now for testing. Going down the 'no comment' route is neither here nor there really, because we have you bang to rights. We're also going over your car while we have it, every nook and cranny."

His head snapped up. "What? Why? What are you trying to do to me?"

"Once we have the results back, then I'll question you again. Until that time, we'll be keeping you here in custody."

Andy stared open-mouthed at his solicitor. "Can she do this?"

"If you're arrested on possession, yes, they have every right to do a thorough search of your vehicle. Is there anything further they're likely to find?"

"No, nothing. Fuck, they've got me by the short and curlies…"

"We have indeed."

"Not you. *They* have."

"Who has, Andy?" Sara jumped in, sensing he was about to make a confession.

"The gang. I didn't want to get involved in any of this. They protected me on the inside and told me I'd have to compensate them for that once I got out."

"By dealing drugs."

"No way, I ain't no dealer."

"Then what are you? What's your part in this?"

"I was supposed to drop the drugs off in town, but your goons jumped me. If they find out about this..."

"What? What have they threatened to do to you, Andy? Or have they got someone else on their radar?"

"Like who?" He gasped when Sara raised her eyebrows. "No, you don't think...?"

She nodded. "Come on. Stop trying to play me."

"I'm not. I swear I'm not. Shit! If they've got Laura...fuck..."

"What are we dealing with here, Andy?"

He shook his head and placed his hands on top. "You don't want to know. They can't be behind her disappearance. They just can't be." His voice trailed off.

"Why not? You had to drop off the package. What would happen if you didn't see that through?"

"They never told me. They knew I would do it for them."

"Think about it, they would've needed some kind of backup plan, isn't that how gangs work?"

"I don't know. This is the first time I've had any dealings with this type of shit." His hands dropped to the table again, and his shoulders slumped. "Fuck...not Laura, this can't be..."

"We can help you get out of this, Andy, if you're willing to trust us."

"Trust you? Why should I? They wouldn't have taken Laura. They would've bloody told me."

"Then who's got her?"

"How the fuck should I know?"

He refused to hold eye contact with her which sparked her suspicion gene into action. *What aren't you telling me, buster?*

"If you're not prepared to work with us, that's the risk you're going to have to take."

"Are you crazy? I said I'd work with you. I'm telling you, they haven't got Laura. I was under no pressure, well, maybe a little, to make the drop-off. If they had Laura, they would've told me, right?"

"Not necessarily. If you're categorically stating the gang haven't got her, then who has?"

"I've told you, I don't frigging know. What if she's done a runner?"

"Why would she?"

"I'm not her keeper, neither am I a fecking mind-reader."

"Sarcasm isn't helping the issue."

"I'm not being sarcastic. Shit, give me a break. I've told you everything I know, and you're still coming down heavy on me. If those drugs don't arrive at the drop-off…"

"What? Come on, you can't leave it there. What are they likely to do?"

He threw his hands up in the air, and they slammed back down on the desk. "Jesus, how many times do I have to say this…? I don't frigging know. Sitting here interrogating me ain't the answer, you need to get off your arses and get out there to look for her."

"Oh, don't worry, my team are doing that all right. We'll see if a spell in a cell will do the trick and loosen that tongue of yours, shall we?"

"Do what you like. Someone is going to need to drop off that gear, otherwise my life ain't gonna be worth living, and that's a fact."

"So you say. I need more than that. Maybe you'll have time to reconsider and think about where they could be holding Laura while you're banged up. Let the duty sergeant know when you're ready to speak to me."

"Is she for real?" he asked his solicitor.

"I have to agree with my client, Inspector. I think you're being unreasonable. He's answered all your questions to the best of his ability."

"Has he? I'm getting the impression he's holding something back. For your information, Miss Clarkson, your client's girlfriend has been missing for over sixty hours now, and I believe your client either has something to do with her disappearance or he knows who is holding her captive."

Miss Clarkson sighed. "I believe my client has told you everything he knows regarding that matter."

"Has he really? I doubt it. Once a con, always a con in my book." *There, I've said it.*

"You're wrong to say that, but I think you know that already, Inspector." Miss Clarkson tucked her legal pad into her briefcase and stood.

"Craig, escort Mr Palmer to his cell, if you would?"

"Yes, boss."

Craig went around the table and pulled Andy to his feet.

Palmer wrenched his arm out of the constable's grasp. "Get your bloody paws off me."

Craig attached his handcuffs to Palmer's wrists and pushed him out of the room.

Sara ran a hand through her blonde hair and winced as she tugged at a knot. "He knows where she is, I'm sure of it."

Miss Clarkson shrugged. "I don't believe he does. He seems genuine enough to me."

"You're wrong. I'd bet my warrant card on it."

"Then we'll have to agree to disagree."

"We will indeed. His car is being processed by forensics. We should know soon enough either way. I'll ring you personally when we have the results back."

"That's kind of you to go out of your way."

"Believe me, it'll be my pleasure."

Sara saw the solicitor back to the reception area and then bolted up the stairs two at a time. "Has anyone got onto the supermarket? I want the footage of the exchange which took place. Let's see him try and squirm his way out of that one. He's not exactly giving us much yet. I can't help thinking there's far more to this than just a drug drop-off."

"I'll get on to that now. Although, Barry and I took down the reg for the gang member's car, so that's a start."

"Excellent. Let's try and rush the results of that through. I have a good feeling about all of this, and I'm determined to keep the momentum going. I'd say I can feel it in my water, except I hate that saying." She laughed and headed for her office to get back to her paperwork.

Craig knocked on her door around forty minutes later.

She sat back and motioned for him to join her, welcoming the breather. "What have you got? Anything?"

"The car is registered to Kevin Prescott. I've run his name through the system and spoken to the detectives who know the gang inside out —actually, that was my first call."

"And?" Sara laced her fingers over her knotted stomach.

"And, he's part of the gang. I have an address for him. What do you want me to do about it?"

"Hang fire for a moment. If this gang has abducted Laura, the last thing we want to do is go in there all guns blazing."

"Okay. Another bout of surveillance then?"

"Possibly. Get back to the detectives first, see if they can give you any possible locations where they could be likely holding her first."

"Will do, boss." He left the room.

She picked up the phone on her desk to check in with her parents to gain some normality in her hectic life.

"Hi, Mum. How are things? Sorry I haven't visited for a week or two."

"Hello, dear. It's two weeks, but who's counting? We're both tickety-boo at this end. Your father is doing so well the doctor has told him that he might be able to come off his medication in a month or two."

Sara gasped. "Wow, that's brilliant news. I'm so pleased for you both. You'll have to make sure he doesn't overdo it in the meantime and set his recuperation back."

"I've threatened him that if he ends up in hospital again, I'll divorce him." Her mother chuckled.

"Yeah, as if that would ever happen. Talking of hospital. I was there last night."

"No! Nothing serious, I hope?"

"Sorry to cause you alarm. No, Mark and I are both well. I received a call from Charlotte, Philip's mother. Her other son, Donald, had a nasty accident. It was touch and go yesterday. He had to undergo major surgery for internal bleeding and he's got several broken bones."

"Oh my, how on earth did that happen?"

"His car hit a lorry, or the other way around, not sure which. It amounted to the same thing, him being admitted with life-threatening injuries."

"His poor mother, I'd be frantic if anything like that ever happened to any of you three," she said, referring to her sister, Lesley, and brother, Timothy, whom Sara had very little to do with—his choice, not hers. "And how is he now, love?"

"I rang the hospital first thing. He's out of ICU and doing as well as can be expected, so that's a blessing."

"Phew, that is good news. He'll have months of recuperating coming his way, won't he?"

"Yep, you're right there."

"How did you get on with his mother?"

"It was all going well until she spotted my engagement ring. It was my fault. I should've taken it off, I just never thought to do it."

"Don't be so ridiculous. She has to accept you're entitled to go on with your life. No parent should expect their loved one's spouse to remain in limbo, mourning them after they're gone."

"I know, Mum. Thanks for reassuring me. It's a good job her husband was there. I think the conversation would've developed differently if he hadn't been."

"You've always been a little wary of her, haven't you?"

Sara laughed. "That's putting it mildly. Anyway, I wanted to bring you up to date with on what's going on at present; don't think I'm avoiding you on purpose. I said I'd go back to the hospital later to check in on him."

"You watch you don't wear yourself out. I know you. Are you working a case at the moment?"

"I am. It's an odd one, a missing person case."

"That's strange for you. I hope you find the person soon."

"Thanks, Mum. I'd better go now. Love to you both."

"Your father and I send you our love, too, sweetie. Take care. Give me a ring when time permits and we'll arrange a get-together in the next few weeks, how's that?"

"Sounds perfect to me. Bye, Mum."

14

"I've told you not to contact me while I'm at work."

"Sorry. I wanted to tell you how it went."

"What went?"

"Setting up Andy Palmer," he told his contact.

"Go on then, I'm up to my eyes in it here."

"Well, I managed to plant the evidence. Made it by the skin of my teeth, too."

"Meaning what? Did he see you?"

"Sort of. Meaning, I followed him to the supermarket. I had no idea he was going to be meeting someone, though. The police were there watching him."

"Shit! They were what? Did they see you?"

"Nah, I dropped the stuff and went into the supermarket to collect a few things. When I came out all hell had let loose. There was a cop car parked in front of his, and Palmer was being put into the back of it. They'd impounded his car as well."

"Oh, my goodness, you've made my day with that news. Top banana, everything is panning out how I planned it, *better* than I planned it even."

"I'm heading out to the barn. You still want me to continue to torture her? She didn't look too good the last time I saw her."

"We've got four days or thereabouts. Yes, continue as instructed."

"Speak soon. Over and out."

He tucked the phone in his pocket and slipped into his car. As usual, he picked up a drive-through meal on the way out to the location.

The girl cowered once the light flooded the barn. He entered, the smell of faeces and urine filling his nostrils the instant he got within ten feet of her. He resisted the urge to heave and placed the food and a bottle of water close to the bags already sitting on the floor. Something caught his eye in the corner of the barn. He could have sworn it was a rat. "I see you have a visitor."

The girl, who appeared exhausted, suddenly sparked into life and turned to look where he was pointing. She screamed, a half-scream anyway—probably that was all she could muster. "Please, you have to let me go. I'm sorry if I've offended you in any way. I didn't mean to. If I have to apologise to everyone else I've upset throughout my life, then so be it, that's what I'm willing to do."

He laughed. "It's too late. Now the critters are here, they'll take care of you. The smell of the food will attract them. The end is nigh, as they say." He spun on his heel and retraced his steps back to the car.

"No! Please, isn't there anything I can do, or say, that will change your mind?"

"Maybe at the beginning I would have been open to having a bit of fun with you. Now, Christ, the thought of laying my hands on you makes me want to bloody vomit. Have fun with your newfound friends." His laughter followed him out of the barn.

15

The results came back sooner than anyone had anticipated. Sara rang Miss Clarkson and asked her to attend another interview with Palmer within the hour. Sara paced her office, livid at what she'd learned, but also elated by the news. It meant they were one step closer to finding Laura Tyler.

At five-thirty, Sara and Carla raced downstairs to find Palmer and his solicitor already sitting at the desk and a uniformed copper standing by the door. Sara acknowledged the constable with a nod.

Carla said what needed to be said to begin the recording, and then Sara began the interview. "Mr Palmer, I'm here to inform you that the forensic results for your vehicle are back. I'm giving you a final opportunity to tell me where Laura Tyler is."

He frowned and slammed back in his chair with enough force that it shifted on the floor. "How many times do I have to fucking tell you? I don't shitting know where she is."

"I think that's bullshit, and I'll tell you why, because I have the evidence that will back up my claim." She grinned at Miss Clarkson whose frown was far deeper than her client's. "First, perhaps you can tell me if Laura has ever travelled in the back of your car. By that, I mean in the boot of the vehicle."

"Are you nuts? Who the fuck would do that?"

"Thank you. Right, maybe you can tell me why forensics found Laura's hair in the boot then?"

"Fuck, are you serious? Maybe it was on my clothes and got in there when I put a bag in the back. Bloody hell, I don't frigging know."

"This wasn't just a single hair. This was a relatively large clump of hair, and that's not all…" She trailed off deliberately.

He tutted noisily. "Go on, the suspense is killing me."

"I bet it is." Sara grinned. "We also found a piece of garment."

"So?"

"This garment happens to be a blouse, the same blouse we have on good authority that Laura was wearing the night she went missing. The day you said you last saw her."

"Fuck off. This is a fucking setup. I know what you lot are capable of. You're fitting me up for something I ain't done. Once a crim, always a crim, right? You'll do anything and everything to get me back behind bars."

"Really? I think you're delusional if you believe that, Mr Palmer. This is your last chance to tell me where you're keeping Laura."

He launched himself forward and slammed his clenched fists onto the table. "I don't know. You can twist this any way you sodding like. I'm telling you, I had nothing, *nothing* to do with her disappearance and I haven't got a clue where she is." There was a noticeable strain in his voice.

Sara was in two minds whether to believe him or not. She kept repeating the same question over and over, trying her hardest to break him down. She showed him the proof of what Laura had been wearing that night from the CCTV footage they had obtained from the college.

He simply shook his head and whispered over and over, "You're wrong. Either you or someone else is setting me up."

Miss Clarkson finally put an end to the interview. "Enough. My client has been fair and open with you. He has repeatedly stated that he has nothing to do with this. Either you charge him with something or let him go."

Sara tilted her head. "Well, okay, it's going to be the former, if you're going to push me into a corner, Miss Clarkson."

Andy quickly glanced at his brief. Eyes wide open, he shook his head. "No, you can't let her charge me. I've done nothing wrong. For God's sake, help me. Do something. Do your bloody job and make her see sense. I can't be banged up again, not for this, not for abducting Laura."

His plea was pitiful.

Miss Clarkson batted the ball in her direction and raised her eyebrows at Sara. "You've heard my client. He knows nothing about his girlfriend's disappearance."

Sara shook her head in disgust. "The evidence is telling me the opposite is true. Where is she, Andy?"

"I don't effing well know. How many more times do I have to tell you that? This is all so wrong. My car has been with you guys for the last what, six or seven hours? Long enough for you to have planted the evidence to make me look bad."

"Whatever, that's not the way we work, especially when we have a missing person on our hands. Come on, admit it, tell us where she is. If you do it now, I'll have a word with the CPS, see if we can do a deal for a lesser charge for you."

He pointed and sneered at Sara. "See, you're admitting your guilt there. Why else would you consider hauling my arse in and offering me a lesser charge?"

"I have to agree with my client, Inspector. Why would you do that?"

She sighed. "We're coming up to Laura being missing for sixty odd hours now. I'm concerned for her safety. As her live-in boyfriend, you should be the same, except all I'm witnessing is signs of anger. Probably because you've been caught out."

"That's bollocks," Andy snapped back.

"Enough. Either charge him or let him go, that's the last time I'm going to say it," Miss Clarkson said, interrupting Sara and Andy's showdown of words.

"I won't be letting you go. We'll be charging you with possession, for now. We'll add to the charges once forensics file their final report and send it to me. Constable, take him back to his cell."

The constable grabbed Andy by the arm and hoisted him out of his seat.

He kicked up a fuss and struck out at the constable. "I'm innocent. Let me go, I've done nothing wrong."

Carla stood and helped the constable get him under control. The three of them left the room.

Sara shook her head. "Innocent my arse. Surely you can see he's responsible for her going missing? My guess is that her body is going to show up soon."

"If he is guilty of abducting her, do you really think it's a good idea to hold him in a cell? Can you afford to have that girl's death on your conscience?"

"No, but what else can I do? He was found in possession of a large amount of drugs. I can't let him off that."

"Then you're in a catch-twenty-two situation, aren't you? Goodbye, Inspector."

Sara walked out with the solicitor, her heart and legs weighted down heavily by the situation. She was not looking forward to her next stop.

"Come in," DCI Price ordered.

Sara tentatively poked her head into the room. "Have you got a few minutes to spare, boss?"

Carol placed her pen on the papers in front of her and slid them to the edge of the desk. Her expression turned to one of concern. "Take a seat, tell me what's on your mind."

Sara rubbed at her chin and sat, nervous about how the conversation would likely go with her superior. "Here's where we stand…" She went through what had occurred in the last few hours.

Carol remained silent throughout, her expression one of thoughtfulness.

"And that's where we're at."

Carol placed her hands up to her face and shook her head. "Shit! You think he's responsible and yet he's denying it, which he's liable to do. How the fuck do we get out of this? What if he's holding her captive somewhere, and we've got him locked up, who is going to feed her in his absence?"

"The same dilemma ran through my mind, and his solicitor's, come to that. What if he has an accomplice?"

"Has he shown any signs of there being one?"

"No, that's the frustrating part. I can't let him go, not now he's been caught in possession of drugs."

Carol rubbed her eye, smearing her mascara in the process. "Damn. You're going to think I'm mad with what I'm about to suggest. What if we let him go and put a tail on him?"

"It's crazy. I can't take the responsibility of having such an action on my shoulders, boss."

"You won't have to. It'll be down to me to accept any blame heading our way. You're doing this as a favour to me, it's only right that I should take the flack for it if things turn sour."

"If you're sure? I did contemplate doing it but thought better of it. It's a tough one."

"As long as we're in agreement that the responsibility falls with me and not you, then do it. You can still lay the drugs charge on him. We wouldn't necessarily keep him locked up for that, would we?"

"I suppose we can release him on an RUI."

Carol nodded thoughtfully. "Yes, that would cover it, Release Under Investigation, yes, do that. Put him under surveillance again, a different car and different officers, maybe a couple of female officers from your team."

"I can do that," she agreed enthusiastically, her own brain whirling with ideas now, proving that coming to see the chief had been the right thing to do. She tapped a pointed finger at her temple. "I'm going to also hold a press conference. I think we need extra help from the general public on this one now. Oh wait, would that be the right thing to do, considering we shouldn't really be tackling this case at all?"

"Do it. The onus will be on me, I can't stress that enough. She's been missing almost three days now, we're entitled to be working this case in the eyes of the law. I'd say even more so now that this new evidence has surfaced."

"I'm worried about that side of things. It's hard keeping all this a secret, boss, truth be told."

"You're coping admirably. Was there anything else?"

"No, I think we've covered everything. I'll charge him with the drug offence then set him free as agreed. Place him on surveillance for the foreseeable future."

Carol shrugged. "If that's the way we have to play it, yes. Let me know the outcome of the press conference. I hope we're not too late and poor Laura is lying buried in a field somewhere."

Sara smiled. "Try not to think about that. I'm not getting the impression that we're too late in the slightest."

"Good. I'll trust your instinct then. Off you pop."

Sara left her seat and returned to the incident room to go over what they had discussed with the team. Marissa and Jill immediately raised their hands to volunteer their services.

"Excellent. I'm going to get our guys to charge him and release him. That's going to take ten to fifteen minutes, so get ready to be in your car within ten minutes, ladies."

The two women gave her the thumbs-up and hurriedly finished off what they were doing. As she made her way into the office, she could hear them going over where they were up to with their research with Carla.

The first person she contacted was the charge sergeant. With the task actioned, her thoughts turned to the press conference, so she rang Jane Donaldson, the press officer, and told her what she needed.

"It's cutting it a bit fine for today. I'll see what I can do for you."

"Thanks, I really appreciate it, Jane. I'd prefer it if there were only a select few there, you know, the local news bods, TV and press."

"Leave me to work my magic and I'll get back to you within thirty minutes, how's that?"

"Sounds perfect to me."

Her final call was to the lab to see how things stood with Palmer's car. They told her that it had been stripped down and would be reassembled the following day. She asked them to make it a priority and explained her intention of putting him under surveillance.

Then she spent the next twenty minutes or so on tenterhooks waiting for Jane to get back to her. Marissa and Jill had already set off, and she was sitting at her desk, willing the phone to ring.

Jane called her back with five minutes to spare of her self-imposed deadline. "Hi, you owe me a drink."

"Gosh, you're a genius. I'll buy you a bottle of the best champers going, via the petty cash, of course."

Jane chortled. "No need, it's my job. We're all set for six o'clock. I don't suppose it will get aired until the late-night news, but it should appear in the press tomorrow."

"You've worked wonders, you never let me down, Jane."

"I do my best. Want me to hang around and be there to support you?"

"No, I'll be fine. You've done enough already. I'll cope on my own, this time."

"Good luck."

"Thanks. Enjoy your evening."

"And you, when you eventually get out of this place."

Sara ended the call and slipped out of the office. "That's all set for six then, the press conference. Any news from the girls yet?"

"They just called in," Carla said. "The sergeant had to call him a taxi. He went straight home."

Sara groaned. "Bugger, I suppose it was to be expected if we've still got his car. He was unlikely to go to the location he's keeping Laura, was he? Or maybe he spotted them on his tail."

"Possibly. Anything else you want us to be getting on with?"

"How are all the background checks coming along?"

"All done as far as I can tell."

"So what else can we look over?"

"Nothing that is coming to mind. We've spoken to everyone we needed to speak to."

Sara sighed and glanced over at the board. She walked forward and cast her eyes over the names again. "The only other doubt in my mind is her boss. What do we know about him, anything?"

Carla's expression didn't exactly fill her with hope. "He seems squeaky clean to me, umm…wrong term if we're to believe they were having an affair, of course, so ignore me. What I meant is that we haven't found any red flags in his past. He's married to Helen Armitage, and they have two sons aged six and eight. They're in a private school."

"Okay, we'll keep him on the backburner for now. I have it in my mind that we should have another word with him. I don't like to think he's going to get away with deceiving us."

"I agree. Shouldn't you be making your way into the lions' den?"

"Shit! I'm out of here. Mustn't keep the press boys waiting. Wish me luck."

"Good luck," Carla shouted after her.

Sara raced down the stairs, furious that time had got away from her at the last minute, preventing her from running a comb through her hair, making herself look presentable for the cameras.

She smoothed down her skirt, adjusted her blouse at the neck and entered the designated conference room. In spite of what Jane had told her, she was surprised to see so many journalists in attendance. Sara began by welcoming them all and thanking them for being there so promptly, then she went through the details of the case they had so far. Her main focus was on the time they believed Laura was picked up by someone, if she was. Once she'd relayed all the information to the sea of faces before her, she prepared herself to be bombarded by questions.

Mike Turnball from the local paper raised his hand first. "DI Ramsey, perhaps you can tell us why you're involved in this case? Don't you generally deal with murder and the heavier types of cases?"

"You're correct, Mike. You know, sometimes police officers work on instinct. This case landed on my desk and instantly piqued my interest. There was nothing more to it than that." She sensed a few pimples breaking out on her tongue because of the white lie she'd been forced to air.

"I see. It's been almost three days now. What are the chances of finding Laura Tyler alive, in your experience?"

"I believe there's every chance of that happening, otherwise I wouldn't be wasting your time with this conference. Truthfully, we're stumped where to turn next, and that's why I'm here, pleading with the public to come forward and help us in our time of need."

A few more hands went up, and she answered their mundane questions as best she could. All she wanted to do now was send the journalists away.

Eventually, once she drew the conference to a halt, her weary legs carried her upstairs. She found the team eager to hear how it went.

"Well, that's done and dusted. Let's go home, guys, and get some rest. Hopefully the phone lines will be red-hot in the morning. Any news from the girls?"

"Nope, he's still there. Maybe it was a waste of time setting up the surveillance, what with him being without a vehicle," Carla announced.

"I agree. A little too hasty to decide that at this stage. I'll get in touch, tell them to go home and rethink things in the morning. Thanks for all your effort today, people. Back to the grind in the morning. Poor Laura will have to spend another night out there, God knows where."

"If she's still alive," Will murmured.

"Not the attitude I was expecting from you, Will. Do you have something on your mind you wish to get out in the open?"

He shook his head. "Sorry to be the one to voice what we're all probably thinking. We're used to cases we can sink our teeth into, boss. This one has been such a chore, I for one, am losing the will to live."

"I completely understand you thinking that way. Let's see what the next couple of days turn up before we consider throwing in the towel, eh?"

"Okay, sorry, boss."

"There's no need for you to apologise, don't think the thought hasn't crossed my mind at all. Stick with it. There's something about this case that is giving me hope. I can't give you more than that at this time."

The team dispersed, and Carla and Sara left the station together.

"What's on your agenda this evening?" Carla asked, halfway down the stairs.

"I'm hoping to go over the wedding plans with Mark, although my head is pounding and telling me that wouldn't be a good idea. What about you?"

"My other half has a late physio appointment. He's hoping to ease back into a few shifts next week, so it'll be feet up for me watching a Netflix series."

"Anything grabbed your attention lately?"

"I've just watched *Safe*, really good, didn't see the ending coming at all."

"Oh, I'll have to look that one up." They reached their cars. "See you in the morning."

"Have a good rest. I sense we're going to be busy tomorrow, or perhaps that's wishful thinking on my part."

Sara held up her crossed fingers and sank her bone-tired body into the car. She started off in the direction of home and slammed the heel of her hand onto the steering wheel as she got close to Roman Road. "Shit, I need to drop by the hospital first. Charlotte and Jonathon will be expecting me." She did a U-turn and headed back into town. En route, she rang Mark's mobile.

"Hey, great minds, I was about to ring you. Are you on your way home?"

"I was, then I remembered I had to call in at the hospital, so I'm going to be late again, love, sorry."

"Damn, I suppose you have a duty to be there for them. Don't worry, I quite understand."

"And that's why I love you so much. It'll be a flying visit, I promise. Have you finished for the night?"

"Yes, just going home now. What do you fancy for dinner?"

"You on a bed of pasta," she retorted quickly, pleased that her brain was functioning and alert.

He laughed. "It could be arranged. I think it would mess up the sheets, though, don't you?"

"Perhaps. In that case, I don't mind, surprise me."

"Okay, I'll do just that. Drive carefully. See you later."

"You will that." She ended the call and rotated the tension out of her neck. Five minutes later, she arrived at the hospital and parked the car.

Charlotte beamed when she saw her and squeezed her in a powerful bear hug.

Jonathon had to step in and encourage his wife to release her grip. "Leave the poor girl be, Charlotte. How are you, Sara?"

"I'm fine. However, I'm not the one lying in a hospital bed. What are you doing out here in the hallway?"

"The nurses asked us to step outside while they change Donald's dressing and give him a bed bath."

"I see. How is he?"

"He woke up at lunchtime but has been drifting in and out all afternoon. They decided to see to him while he was awake rather than disturb his sleep. We're hopeful he's going to make a full recovery, though," Charlotte rambled, using every inch of breath lying stagnant in her lungs.

"That's great news. You must both be pleased with his progress?"

"We are." Jonathon hugged her. "We can't thank you enough for coming here. We still regard you as part of this family, we always will," he whispered in her ear.

Tears sprang to her eyes, and she pecked him on the cheek. "I still feel like I belong. I hope that doesn't change in the future, you're all a very special part of my life."

"What a lovely thing to say." Charlotte withdrew a tissue from her sleeve and dabbed at her eyes and her nose.

She smiled and patted Charlotte's forearm, comforting her. "Has he spoken yet? Does he know who you are? Or is it too soon for that?"

"No, he hasn't spoken. We haven't pushed it either. He'll speak when he wants to. Will you stay with us, come in and see him once the nurses give us the all clear?" Jonathon replied.

"Of course. I'm not in any rush to get home." She cursed herself for telling them a huge lie. She was eager to get home and be with her fiancé after her troublesome day at work. "Can I get either of you a drink?"

"You stay here, I'll get them," Jonathon piped up.

"Thanks, a coffee with one sugar for me please," Sara replied.

"I'll pass this time around. I don't fancy another trip to the loo so soon after the last one."

Jonathon wound his way down the hallway, leaving her alone with Charlotte. By the determined expression that developed on her former mother-in-law's face, she could tell she was in for a quick-fire round of questions in her husband's absence.

"When are you due to get married?"

"We're still deciding on a date, Charlotte. I should be at home now, planning my wedding, but I'm here with you guys."

Charlotte seemed taken aback by her admission. "Oh, really. Sorry if we've inconvenienced you at all, Sara," she replied tartly.

Fuckity fuck, I had to reveal more than she asked for, didn't I?

"It's fine, we'll probably sit down at the weekend to cement the details. Donald's welfare is my priority at present."

"I'm glad to hear it." Charlotte heaved out a breath, and tears dripped down her flushed cheeks. "I'm sorry. I know you have a life of your own to consider and I really do appreciate you being here with us, it proves how much we mean to you…"

Sara sensed a *but* coming…

"But, I don't mind telling you that I had high hopes of you and Donald getting together, once upon a time."

Sara's eyes widened before she had the chance to stop them. "I don't think that was ever on the cards, Charlotte, not for me, anyway."

"He's got a crush on you, or he had, before his accident. He'd be mortified to know you're engaged. I wonder if I can ask you to remove your ring before we go in there to see him."

"What would be the sense in doing that?"

"To save him from getting upset, dear. You understand, don't you?"

She knew Donald liked her, they'd shared a kiss not long after Philip had died, so that much was evident, but would it be right to deceive him now? There were a dozen pros and cons running through her mind to executing Charlotte's request. Luckily, Jonathon reappeared with their drinks and deterred her from answering.

"Everything all right?" he asked suspiciously, his gaze flicking between them.

"Of course it is, we were having a nice chat about your work, weren't we, dear?" Charlotte answered quickly.

"Yes. I have a tough few days ahead of me. Therefore, I'll need to shoot off once I've said hello to Donald." *Phew! Back of the net, girlie. That'll put her in her place, no doubt.*

"That's a shame, isn't it, Charlotte. You mustn't think badly about it, though, Sara, we realise how busy you are and appreciate you going out of your way to come here when you should be resting at home with your young man."

Charlotte's glare in her direction intensified along with the colour in her cheeks.

Sara smiled at both of them and removed the lid off her coffee. "Cheers. Here's to Donald making a full recovery."

"I'll drink to that," Jonathon replied, sipping from his drink.

After that, Jonathon kept the conversation going between them. He was a keen golfer and for the next fifteen minutes he regaled them with stories about the luxury resorts he'd played at over the years until a nurse came to rescue her.

The three of them entered the ward. Sara's gaze was like a laser, fixed on Donald during the measured walk to his bed. He didn't turn to face them. Instead, he stared ahead at the unconscious patient opposite who was being attended to by two nurses.

"Hello, love, look who's come to visit you. It's Sara."

His head slowly turned in her direction. Sara glimpsed a spark of recognition in his eyes. She smiled. He blinked a few times and then rested his head back against the pillows.

"Hello…Sara…you…came…" His speech was slow, and he paused heavily between each word.

Charlotte slammed a hand over her mouth and whimpered. Jonathon placed an arm around her shoulders. Sara took a step closer to the bed and studied Donald. His face was black and blue around the eyes, and his nose was set differently to how she remembered it, but it was the bandage to his head which worried her the most. She swallowed down the bile burning her throat and laid a hand over one of his. A glimmer of a smile touched his lips but soon evaporated.

"How are you, Donald?"

"Fine…"

"That's good to hear. Fancy you having an argument with a lorry. What was that all about?"

His smile reappeared and vanished just as quickly. His eyes flickered shut again, and within seconds his breathing had altered. He'd dropped off to sleep. Jonathon guided his wife back into the hallway.

Sara leaned forward and pecked Donald on the cheek. "Wishing you well, Donald. You'll pull through this, you have the strength and the determination to prove me right."

He snored gently in response. She left his side and returned to the hallway to find Charlotte sitting in a chair, sobbing.

She crouched in front of her and placed her hands over Charlotte's. "Don't go getting yourself worked up, he's strong, he'll get through this."

"He sounds different. As though his brain is damaged…" More sobs.

"Please, don't upset yourself. You're going to need to speak to the doctor. Don't let your imagination run wild without having all the facts to hand."

Charlotte looked up. "But you heard him. And why hasn't he spoken to us, his parents?"

"I can't answer that, Charlotte. Don't tear yourself up about this. Speak to the doctor, voice your concerns with him."

"I will, don't you worry. Don't you have a fiancé to go home to?"

Sara stood, dumbstruck by the venom in her words. She glanced at Jonathon who shrugged.

"Maybe it's time you went, love."

"Okay, if that's what you want. I'm glad he's regained consciousness. Will you ring me, keep me abreast of his recovery and what the doctor tells you?"

"We will. Thanks for coming, Sara, we always value the time you spend with our family." Jonathon leaned forward and kissed her on the cheek.

"Goodbye, Charlotte."

"Bye," she mumbled without any eye contact.

Sara left the hospital, pondering what she had done wrong. She drove home in a daze. Mark picked up that something was wrong the moment she walked through the front door. By the way she scooped Misty up and buried her face in her cat's fur.

"Everything all right?"

"I'm fine. Leave it for now, I need to process it all before I talk about it. I'm not blocking you out, I promise." She walked towards him and kissed him.

"I'm here when you need me. Do you want some dinner?"

"Why not? What's on the menu?"

"Pork chops, mashed potatoes and greens."

"You're an absolute treasure, thank you for taking care of me."

"We take care of each other and we always will in the future."

"I hope so." She lowered Misty to the floor and went upstairs to get changed. By the time she came back downstairs, the events which had taken place at the hospital were a distant memory that she'd successfully pushed aside.

Mark didn't bother revisiting the subject the rest of the evening. She was grateful for his sensitivity. When they went to bed, he held her tightly, and that was when she broke down and revealed the truth. He listened intently, refusing to judge Donald's mother for lashing out. But that was Mark all over…and the reason why she loved him so much.

16

Sleep came in fits and starts during the night. Sara left the house at her normal time, Mark seeing her off at the front door for a change as he wasn't due in until late morning. He had an operation to do at seven that evening so wouldn't be home until around ten. She'd miss him, at least, she had an idea she might. There was no telling how her own day would pan out in the meantime.

She tapped her fingers on the steering wheel. The slight traffic jam she found herself stuck in was usual for this time of day, even on a Saturday. It was her team's turn to cover the weekend. She could see the top floors of the station ahead of her, within spitting distance. *So near and yet so far!*

Eventually, she drew into her allocated space and entered the station. "Hi, Jeff. How's it going?"

"Morning, boss. There are a few messages on your desk."

"Anything of interest?"

He hitched up a shoulder and smiled. "Maybe."

"Bloody tease." She bolted through the door and up the stairs to the incident room. "Morning, team, I'll be with you in a tick."

A chair scraped, and not long after, Carla appeared in the doorway of her office. "Morning. Everything all right?"

"I'll let you know once I've read these notes." She flicked through them and plucked out one that caught her eye. She passed it across the table for Carla to read.

"What? Why didn't she bloody tell us this at the time?"

"Exactly. I'm going to give her a call now. Apart from this little lot, have any other calls of interest come in yet?"

"No, nothing."

"Okay, I'll deal with this and let you know what she has to say for herself. I can bloody do without this shit to start the day on."

Carla left her to it.

She collapsed into her chair, cleared her throat then made the call. "Hi, Cassandra. It's DI Sara Ramsey. You left a message for me to ring you."

"I did. I probably should have mentioned it before; it slipped my mind when you were here."

"Never mind. What can you tell me about this ex-boyfriend?"

"He started stalking her. You know the type, refused to take no for an answer. Look, I might be speaking out of turn and he may not have anything to do with her disappearance, I just thought you should know."

"Always good to hear about things of this ilk. When was the last time Laura had any dealings with this David Powell?"

"Off the top of my head I would say it has to be a couple of years ago, although he tends to send her a card on her birthday and for Christmas."

"Creepy. I don't suppose you know where I'm likely to find this guy?"

"The last I heard he was in Birmingham. Where exactly, is anyone's guess."

"Okay. One last thing. Was Laura ever scared of this man? Either when they were together or after they broke up?"

"She had her reservations about him while they were dating. He'd show up to check on her when she was on a night out with the girls, that sort of thing."

"And was it the same story after they broke up?"

"For a while, yes."

"And what happened to alter that?"

"She had to threaten him, make him back away."

Sara perched on the edge of her seat. "Threaten him? How?"

"She threatened that she would go to the police. All went quiet after that. Like I said when I rang, it might be something and nothing. His name came into my mind last night while I was watching the news. I take it she hasn't been found yet?"

"That's correct. Okay, thanks for getting in touch, I'll look into it today. Are you sure there's nothing else you can think of that will help the investigation?"

"Nope, sorry. I know I should've thought about telling you sooner. My mistake."

"Thanks for getting in touch." She ended the call and left the office. "Okay, interesting titbit for us to explore. Christine, I'd like you to find out what you can about a David Powell. That's all I have on him, except his last known address was in Birmingham. Apparently, Laura used to go out with him. He was the possessive type, stalkerish even, during and after their relationship."

"I'll try and find him, boss."

"Good. I need us all to be prepared to man the phones today, although, Jill and Marissa, I'd still like you to go out on surveillance. Bear with me on that one. I'm going to have to ring the lab to see when his car is likely to be released."

"No problem," Jill replied.

"Boss, I've got two David Powells in the Birmingham area for you," Christine called over.

"That was quick. Can you narrow it down by their ages?" Sara approached Christine's desk.

"I'll try. Ah, here we are. The first is sixty-six, and the other is thirty-five."

"The latter sounds more plausible. See what you can find out about him for me, please, Christine."

"Give me ten minutes."

The phone rang on Will's desk, followed by another call coming in for Craig to answer. Sara eyed Carla with optimism. Was this a sign of things to come for the day? She hoped so. The first few calls proved to be hopeless. Do-gooders trying to make a name for themselves and supplying either false or irrelevant information to do with the case.

Christine left her desk and handed her a sheet of paper. The efficient constable had found out what she could about David Powell, which included the fact he worked for the railway as a ticket collector.

"Interesting. Could that mean he travels down to this neck of the woods?"

"Want me to place a call, see what I can find out?" Christine asked.

"Do it. We've got nothing else to go on, however, the calls appear to be coming in now. Dare I say it? I have a good feeling that something significant is going to come our way today. The question is, from which direction?"

Christine drifted back to her desk, and Sara circulated the room, listening to her team's conversations with the general public who had gone out of their way to contact them.

Carla clicked her fingers to gain Sara's attention and beckoned her over.

"What is it?" Sara mouthed.

"Okay, sir. You mentioned you saw a man picking up a young woman that evening. Can you tell me what type of car it was?" Carla put the phone on speaker.

"A dark one. Sorry, I'm no good with makes and models, I just drive the damn things. My son's the enthusiast in the family. Me, I'd rather spend my time perfecting my golf swing than diving under the bonnet of a car."

Carla rolled her eyes and rubbed the side of her face with her pen. "That's a shame. Was it a four-by-four or an estate car for instance?"

"Couldn't tell you. It was dark, and it was sheeting it down."

"I know your intention is good, but it's no good to us if you can't provide us with something else, sir."

"Don't you have a go at me, young lady, I'm doing my best here, trying to help you."

"I know that and appreciate it, sir. Is there anything else you can tell me about the car?"

"I saw some of the registration number, but you're not likely to be interested in some of it, are you?"

"On the contrary, sir. Something is better than nothing, we can still work with that."

"It was JD 34…if that helps?"

"It does. Can you tell me if the young woman got into the vehicle of her own accord, or did the man force her to get in?"

"Oh no. He pulled up alongside her; she was walking. Looked like a drowned rat, she did. She bent down to speak to him through the window and then got in. I passed by around about then and carried on down the road."

"Did you see them drive away?"

"I did. He followed me down the road and around the roundabout."

"Going in which direction?"

"Towards Worcester. I tend to put my foot down, sticking to the fifty miles per hour speed limit, of course, so I can't tell you where they went from there."

"You didn't see them again? Not in your rear-view mirror at all?"

"Nope, I would have told you if I had. That's all I've got for you. I told you it wouldn't be of much use."

"You're wrong, sir, the information you've given me has been valuable. We have something to go on now. It might not be much but it's more than we had before you called us. Thank you."

"It is? Well, that is good news. I'm sorry I didn't contact you sooner in that case. It was seeing it on the news last night that jolted my memory."

"Thanks for contacting us."

"You're welcome." He hung up.

Sara high-fived Carla. "This could be the break we've been looking for. Can you run the plate for me?"

"On it now. I'm hopeful we can get something from this. It's about time things started to go our way."

Sara continued circulating the room.

Christine reported back to her within a few minutes. "Boss, I have something, but it's not what you want to hear."

Sara's heart sank, her recent euphoria shattered to tiny pieces. "Go on, give it to me."

"Powell generally works on the line heading north and not south."

"Not what I was hoping to hear."

"I know, I'm sorry. Does that mean you want to draw a halt to this line of enquiry now?"

"Not just yet. Can you do me a favour and find out what car he has registered in his name? It could be important."

Christine nodded and pounded her keyboard. "I have it. An older vehicle, registration BS—"

Sara held up her hand, she'd heard enough. "Okay, I don't think it's him. We'll still add his name to the list if the other line of enquiry dries up. Talk about highs and lows within a few minutes. Still, mustn't grumble, at least we have more information than we started out with this morning."

Carla followed her into her office moments later. "It's a local plate. There are around ten cars beginning with JD 34 in the immediate area."

"Bugger." Sara kicked out at the spare chair sitting in the corner and focussed her attention on the view out of her window, hoping it would have the usual effect of calming her down. "Okay, let's whittle that list down and see what surfaces, Carla. I'm going to ring the lab about Andy's car. At least we know he was telling us the truth. However, that also bloody muddies the water, doesn't it?"

"The evidence leads us to believe it was him, but we have witness' statements telling us otherwise—he was at the pub at the time she got picked up."

"Ain't that the bloody truth? So, where does that leave us? Is someone frigging messing with us? He swore blind he didn't have anything to do with the evidence being in his vehicle. About that... How would a thick clump of hair be in the boot of his car anyway? The odd hair I can accept."

Carla nodded. "Sounds like he's being framed to me. But why? Is it the gang pulling his strings? Could they have her, forcing him to play by their rules and deliver the drugs for them?"

"It's the only thing I can think of. Let's see what Jill and Marissa come back with. I'll make the call, get the ball rolling."

"I'll get you a coffee, you look as if you could do with one."

Sara nodded. "Thanks, partner." She rounded the desk, dropped into her chair and rang the lab.

Colin Frasier answered the call. "Hi, I was just about to ring you."

"About anything in particular?"

"Nope, only to say the car has been put back together and we're ready to hand it over to you now."

"Brilliant. Did you find anything else?"

"Nothing. Only the hair and the fabric sample."

"About that, I've been thinking and could do with your expert opinion on my thoughts."

"Sounds ominous. Hit me with it."

"How often do you come across large clumps of hair like that when you examine a suspect's car?"

"Hmm...I have to be honest and tell you rarely, if at all, especially hair that's been cut."

"Thanks for confirming my suspicions."

"Which are?"

"That Palmer has been set up."

"Heck, are you telling me my team and I busted a bloody gut for nothing?"

Sara cringed, hunching her shoulders up to her ears. "I wouldn't necessarily say it was a waste of your time."

"I would. If you had thoughts along those lines, the least you could've done was mentioned it from the outset."

"I didn't. It's only been in the last few hours that it's occurred to me. I would never waste your valuable time intentionally."

He grunted. "I bet. I'm disappointed in you, Inspector. Don't expect a favour from me in the future, not if you have a problem being honest with me. I'll get one of my guys to drop the car back ASAP." He slammed the phone down, the sound ringing in her ear.

"Shit! Well, that was bloody uncalled for. Me and my big mouth. Why can't I keep it shut?"

Carla entered the room to find Sara cradling her head in her hands.

"What's wrong? It's not your ex-brother-in-law, is it?"

"No. Sorry, it's me overreacting. Colin at the lab just tore me off a strip when I raised my reservations about the evidence found in Palmer's car, that's all. He threw a fit, told me if I suspected Palmer had been set up, I should've mentioned it from the get-go."

"That's nuts. Don't listen to him. It's not relevant. Don't let him upset you. We have everything going in our favour now, don't let someone put a dampener on your morale."

"You're right. Screw him. Anyway, he told me he was about to release Palmer's vehicle. I'll ring Palmer, let him know that we'll arrange for the vehicle to be brought back here and he can come and collect it sometime today. Then we'll see where he goes from there."

"That's leaving me scratching my head. You're still going to put a tail on him even though you think he's been set up?"

"We have to, it's all we have at the moment. What if this has nothing to do with the gang? I've had time to reflect on that aspect. Think about it logically. Why would the gang set him up if they intend using him to ferry the drugs?"

Carla cupped her chin between her finger and thumb. "I get you. It doesn't make sense. It only makes my head hurt more, truth be told."

"Yeah, you and me both. I don't know if we're doing the right thing or not, but that's the only option I can see we have at present."

"Who knows how these gangs work? I still can't fathom why they would set him up."

"I know. It's a mess. The more I think about it, the more unlikely I believe it is. Okay, look at it this way. Someone got close enough to his car to plant that evidence. Maybe they'll try again."

Carla nodded slowly. "Now that makes more sense."

"Let me ring him." She picked up the phone and arranged for Palmer to come in around an hour later.

He seemed relieved to be getting his vehicle back.

"I'll be there," he told her and then hung up.

*A*ndy Palmer arrived at the station. Marissa and Jill jumped into action and followed him for most of the day. They reported in a few times with very little information. Once he'd left the station, he went straight home. At two p.m., he took off and met up with a couple of men, who were built like bouncers, at a scrapyard.

Sara got the team digging as to who owned the yard, in case Laura was possibly being kept there. The research came back that it was a legitimate business and nothing to do with the gang Palmer was working with.

Then Palmer stopped off at the supermarket, shopped for twenty minutes and returned to his car carrying two bags laden with what appeared to be tinned goods, probably lagers or beers, Will had suggested.

With very little else to report, Sara's anxiety rose up the levels until she found herself chewing the skin around her thumb, enough to make it bleed. Something was niggling at her gut about this whole setup.

"Craig, do me a favour. Have we still got that CCTV footage from Sainsbury's?"

"Yep, I've got it on my computer. Want me to bring it up on the screen, boss?"

"If you would. I'll be with you in a moment. Actually, can you dash out and get some sandwiches?"

"Of course."

"Here's a twenty. I'll have an egg mayo on brown, thanks."

Craig went around the room taking down the orders, then left.

"What are you thinking?" Carla asked, interrupting her thoughts.

"I don't know. I'm digging more out of hope than anything. Maybe searching for the impossible, something that will trigger sending us in the right direction for a change instead of going round and round in a bloody circle. I'm glad the chief hasn't visited us today. I feel shit enough about not finding Laura by now without her breathing down my neck."

"Has she come down heavy on you?"

Sara shook her head. "No. Damn, ignore me, it was remiss of me to say that."

17

*P*lease, won't someone come and help me? I've spent the last couple of days, maybe more—I have no concept of time any longer—repenting my sins. I was wrong to have continually set out to hurt people with my lies. I wasn't aware of the damage I was causing. If only I could face all the people I've hurt over the years and tell them how much I regret what I've done. But, surely, I don't deserve this. To be treated as an animal without basic necessities.

A noise rustled behind her. She screamed. It usually did the trick to keep the rats at bay, however, they still managed to get to the food. To drag parts of it away to their lair, tucked behind the bale of straw she was lying on. Being aware how close they were, prevented her from closing her eyes. She was exhausted, her stomach painful where the hunger pangs tore through her. Her head pounded from the worst headache imaginable. Her hands shook. Her lips were sore, cracked and bleeding at times through lack of water.

Every shadow turned her imagination upside down. She caught herself hallucinating. Visualising banquets of food and lashings of champagne to quench her thirst. When she tried to reach for a glass, her hand slipped through the stem. Was this the man's intention? To torture her day and night without actually laying a finger on her?

Tears slid down her cheeks. "I can't cope any more. Please, God, take me now before I have to go through much more of this hell on earth."

She'd been so wrapped up in her thoughts and fending off her furry company that she'd neglected to hear the car arrive. The opening of the barn door startled her. She blinked against the bright daylight. The man's outline was like a hazy vision. *Is he another hallucination?*

He marched towards her. In his hand, the usual paper McDonald's bag and a bottle of water. He placed it on the floor, surveyed the food that was already in situ and glared at her. "Have you touched this?"

"No. How could I? It's out of my reach. The rats, they come out of their hidey-holes and take it back with them. I'm scared of them. Please, won't you consider letting me go?" she pleaded, showing how much little self-respect she had left.

He tipped back his head and roared with laughter then glared at her. "You think this is supposed to be some kind of holiday camp, with all mod cons and amenities? In your dreams. This is supposed to be a punishment. For you to contemplate your life and what a dumb bitch you've been over the years. Is it true, about your father? Or was that one of your many lies?"

Her head dipped, shame instantly replacing her feistiness. "Yes," she uttered.

"That's bollocks. You see, I know all about you and what you've been guilty of in the past. How could you do that to your own father?"

"I didn't. You don't understand. No one will ever understand." Her voice trailed off. Talking considerably hurt her throat which was dry to the point of bleeding.

"Don't I? I understand enough to know the type of person I'm dealing with. You disgust me. To accuse your father of…abusing you. You wouldn't know what abuse was if it slapped you in the face." He lifted his T-shirt to show her the scars slashed across his torso. "That's abuse. Take it from someone who genuinely knows what a father's hatred feels like."

"I'm sorry."

He leaned in then retreated, the smell of her bodily fluids making him repel. "You have no idea what it was like, living in fear as a child. Hiding under the covers in case either your father or your mother came into your room for a quick grope. And you have the audacity to make things up about your own father. The damage you caused to your parents' marriage, and still you never learnt. You persisted in ruining other people's lives with your lies and underhand treatment. Go on, admit it, it's still going on today, isn't it? Aren't you shagging your married boss now?"

"No," she replied without conviction.

"Liar," he sneered venomously.

She looked to the side, too embarrassed to hold his stare. "I'm sorry. I could apologise to everyone, if that's what you want me to do," she croaked, swallowing hard to replace the saliva.

"It's too late for that. The decision has been made." He turned and left the barn.

She reached out with both arms, her pleas going unheard. *I don't want to die, not like this. What will the rats do once all the food has gone, start on me? Will I survive that long? How long will I survive without food and water? I don't know. Nor do I wish to know. Take me now, let's get this over with, God. Do it!*

18

The team sat with a coffee and ate their lunch. It had been a hectic and tension-filled morning for all of them. Now the phones had died down there was every hope that the afternoon would bring the results Sara was after. Marissa and Jill were still out on the road, watching Palmer's every move. Nothing to mention there, after he'd gone back home.

After eating his sandwich, Craig set up the footage and flicked through the shots until he reached the part where he and Barry had blocked Palmer's path in the car park and made the arrest.

"Wind it back, let's see what we can find," Sara requested. She inched forward on the desk she was perched on. "Go back to where Palmer arrived, will you?"

The picture rewound at speed, and Craig halted it where Palmer entered and parked his car. Another couple of cars came in immediately after him. One of those vehicles parked opposite his.

Craig tapped the screen with his finger. "We presumed he was meeting this guy at first."

"Oh, did he have a conversation with him?"

"No, he ended up walking past his car."

Sara's eyes narrowed. "Take it back. Can you slow it down a little?"

Craig did as instructed, and they both edged forward to scrutinise the images closely.

"His hands, is he holding something?" Craig pointed at the screen.

"Can you freeze it and zoom in, Craig?"

"There, isn't that the same coloured fabric the lab found?"

Sara punched the air and gripped his shoulder. "I do believe you're right. Continue running it."

The man went past Palmer's car and into the store.

"He walked in as if he didn't have a care in the world."

"Okay, now take it right back, let's see what car he's driving."

Craig nodded and whizzed the footage back to where Palmer entered the car park again five minutes or so earlier. He slowed it down intentionally and then pointed to the three cars which followed the suspect in.

"Humour me; zoom in on the number plates."

Craig hit a button on the keyboard, and the picture shifted to focus on the plates.

"Oh my giddy aunt, will you look at that?" Sara pointed at the dark car. "JD 34 SYN. Christine, go through that list of reggies you've got. Is there a JD 34 SYN on it?"

Christine swiftly searched the data she had and whooped. "It's here. The car belongs to a Calum Richardson."

Sara breathed out a sigh of relief. "Shit! At last we're finally getting somewhere. Carla, fancy sitting in the car for a few hours?"

"I don't mind, as long as it results in an arrest."

"There's every possibility. Christine, give Carla the address. I'm going to run this past the chief before she jumps down my throat for not keeping her up to date on things. I'll be right back. Get ready to shoot off."

The chief turned out to be as excited as Sara, but even then, she urged Sara not to screw things up and do something that could possibly put Laura's life in danger.

Sara asked the chief to trust her, and she returned to the incident room to collect Carla on the way out of the station.

"Where am I heading?"

"Broomy Hill, Barton Road."

"Do I need the satnav, or do you know where that is?" Sara asked, selecting first gear and tearing out of the car park.

"I know. Head for the hospital, and I'll give you pointers from there."

"You realise this could be it?"

"Is it worth adding a note of caution? Will you even listen to me?" Carla replied.

Sara grinned and wrinkled her nose. "Let's see if I'm right first and then go from there. Did Christine manage to find out much about him?"

"He's a delivery driver of sorts. Not your usual type. He picks up medicines from a pharmacy and delivers them to the local people who are unable to collect them."

"Interesting. Palmer's a delivery driver as well. So does this mean Richardson likely drives another vehicle? Might be something to be aware of," Sara replied.

"Right, so he might not be at home now, is that what you're saying?"

"Yep, that's the way I'm thinking. Get Christine to ring the pharmacy, see if he's on duty today."

Carla made the call and waited for Christine to get back to her. "He's on a week's holiday."

Sara glanced at Carla and cocked one of her eyebrows. "Really? That's interesting."

They parked several feet from number ten Barton Road and settled down for the long haul. His car was outside the property. They waited and waited, and still nothing until dusk fell, then Richardson appeared and jumped in his car.

"I'll keep my distance, let a car or two in between just in case." Sara followed him through the town and past the college where Laura worked. "Let's see if he takes the same route the witness said he took on the night in question."

He did. They travelled along the A4103 towards Worcester, their speed increased. Suddenly, he indicated and took the A465.

"Going out to Bromyard, right?"

"So it would seem," Carla agreed.

They reached the village of Burley Gate. Richardson turned into a small road.

Fearing he might see them, Sara drove past. "Could you make anything out?"

"It appeared to be a track of sorts. Can you pull over and we'll wait it out? Or find an adjacent track where we can go on foot?"

"That's more like it." Sara's stomach was somersaulting at this point, her breathing coming in quick short bursts as adrenaline rushed through her veins. She pulled over in a lay-by.

Carla was fiddling with her phone. She angled it towards Sara. "I've got Google Maps. I think that's the lane there." She fiddled again and showed Sara the screen. "There's a barn up there. And what looks to be a derelict farmhouse."

"Plausible, right?"

"I should say so."

Sara bashed the steering wheel. "It's too dark to track him on foot."

"Is it?" Carla grinned, waving her trusty phone in her hand. "Phones come with torches nowadays."

"Smartarse. Come on, I'm game if you are?"

"Too right."

They left the car and jogged back to the lane. Carla shone the torch on the ground in front of them, and they raced to the top of the slight incline. They hugged the hedge once the car came into sight. The barn door was open. Sara gestured for them to keep to the grass verge and off the slight gravelled area. They pressed themselves against the side of the barn. Sara pointed out a gap in the cladding. She peered through it and saw Richardson bending over, talking to someone. When he stood erect again, Sara gasped.

"Oh, God, it's her. Bloody hell, we've found her."

"Jesus, she's still alive?"

"Yes, but she doesn't look good. Ssh...he's coming. Take some photos of his car, we'll need it as evidence."

Richardson padlocked the barn again and drove off.

"He'll fucking keep. We need to get in there and rescue her."

"How? Do you have any bolt cutters in the car?"

"No. Shit, call for backup. Ring Barry, I'm sure he'll have some, he's got tons of useless stuff in his boot."

Carla rang the station and asked to be put through to Barry. She explained the situation and what their location was, asked him to join them ASAP and then ended the call.

"He'll be here in twenty minutes."

"Okay, we're going to have to stay hidden, in case he comes back. I need to speak to her, though, tell her we're here and that she's safe."

"Do you want me to ring for an ambulance, if you think she's that bad?"

"Leave it for now. We have to go past the hospital on our way back, it'll probably be quicker to take her ourselves. There's the added problem that he might return. I'd hate a paramedic to get caught up in any aggro."

"Okay, I get that."

Sara moved down to the bottom of the barn. A rat scurried across her path, and she shrieked.

"Who's there?" Laura shouted, her voice faint.

"Laura Tyler, my name is Sara Ramsey. I'm a police officer. You're safe. We're going to get you out of there."

"How? When? What if...?"

"Leave all that up to us. The man has gone. How often does he come to check on you?"

"Sometimes twice a day. He's been twice already. Help me. The rats. I'm so scared of the rats."

"Don't worry. I'll make some noise to deter them from coming near you." She hated the critters herself, but that didn't matter. Nothing mattered except rescuing Laura.

Fifteen minutes later, Barry screeched to a halt in front of the barn. Sara had never been so relieved to see someone in all her life.

"Get it open, Barry."

He leapt out of the car, followed by Craig. "I'll do my best, boss."

He made short work of breaking open the padlock and pushed the door open for Sara and Carla to race inside.

"We'll still need them, she's got a chain around her middle."

"Rightio." Barry marched after them.

Sara was tempted to hold her nose against the smell emanating from the damsel in distress, but she resisted.

Barry did the necessary and stood back. Laura sobbed and fell against Sara. She offered the woman a bottle of water which she gulped down in one go.

"Steady, take it easy."

"I thought I was going to die. He refused to give me food and water."

"I can see that. Did he say why he was holding you?"

"He kept mentioning the lies and the disruption I had caused to peoples' families. I told him I would try and make amends, but he insisted it wouldn't be enough. He was going to let me die."

"Let's get you up. Can you stand? Barry, help me get her to her feet."

Barry hopped around the other side, and together they eased her into position. It was obvious how weak she was. Her legs gave way beneath her within seconds. Barry, being the gent he was, and in spite of the mess Laura was in, hoisted her into his arms and took her out to the car.

"Mine or yours, boss?"

"Mine. Wait. I have a plastic sheet in the boot, I'll get that. No offence, Laura."

"None taken. I feel ashamed of what he's done to me."

Once they had Laura settled in the back seat, they set off for the hospital. During the journey, Sara kept up her questions—there were so many running through her mind. The most important of which was, "Do you know him?"

Laura shook her head. "No, I've never laid eyes on him before. Which was totally confusing for me."

"Did he mention working with someone else?"

"No, not that I can remember. What if he tracks me down and comes after me again?"

"He won't, we're going to arrest him now. Carla, now Laura's safe, place the call."

"On it. Do you want me to ring Lin and the chief as well?"

"If you would, thanks."

At the mention of her mother's name, Laura broke down in tears.

"It's all right, Laura. You're safe, there's no need for you to worry any more."

"I feel so guilty…of the way I've treated people over the years. If I hadn't been such a bitch, this would never have happened."

"Okay, if we're thinking along those lines, is there anyone out there who you've hurt enough who might want to do this to you? We've questioned everyone we can think of who you're connected to, at least we think we have. The only one we haven't managed to speak to is David Powell."

Laura stopped crying and gasped. "Oh my God, yes, it could have been him. He was really creepy, stalked me for a while until I warned him to back off."

"But he took the hint, right?"

"He did, at the time. What if his infatuation with me started up again?"

"I'll be honest with you, the reason we discounted him was because of the number plate we ran. It belonged to Calum Richardson, the man who was holding you. My dilemma is, if you don't know him, he must have a connection to someone else you do know."

"So David could be behind it after all."

"Okay, yes, he might. Richardson should be picked up soon. We'll see what he has to tell us under caution. Let's leave the questions for now, we're almost at the hospital."

"Thank you for rescuing me. I'm not sure how much longer I would've lasted in that hellhole."

"We did our best, we would never have given up on you. Not with the chief breathing down our necks anyway."

"Okay, that's all taken care of. Lin and the chief are both on their way and will meet us at the hospital," Carla announced.

"Great stuff. All's worked out well in the end. We just need to question Richardson, to see what his motive was or find out who's pulling his strings."

Carla's mobile rang and she answered it. "Good. We should be back at the station soon. Throw him in a holding cell until we get there." She ended the call and punched the air. "They've got him."

Sara expelled a large breath. "Thank fuck for that."

Not long after, they arrived at the hospital. Sara sent Carla to collect a wheelchair for Laura. She tried to insist she could walk but collapsed after taking a few fragile steps. Sara wheeled her into the Accident and Emergency Department and informed the doctor about the circumstances behind her admittance. He was appalled by her plight and promised to take care of her straight away.

Carla bought them both a coffee from the small café, and they waited patiently for Lin and the chief to arrive. The pair of them burst through the doors together around fifteen minutes later.

"How is she?" Carol Price asked breathlessly.

"The doctor's checking her over now. She appears to have something wrong with her shoulder and a possible broken nose. Apart from that, she seems to be in good spirits, relieved that we found her. She's pretty weak from lack of food. There was food there, but it was deliberately placed out of her reach."

"What? Who would be so cruel as to do that?" Carol scowled.

"We've got her abductor in custody. Now you're here, Carla and I are going to head back to base to interview him, if that's okay with you guys?"

"Of course it is. Go, give him hell. Keep me informed," Carol instructed.

"I will."

Lin offered a weak smile. "I can't thank you enough for finding her, thank you."

Sara laid a hand on her arm. "You're welcome. Take care of her."

Then Sara and Carla raced out of the hospital and headed back to the station.

"Where is he?" Sara asked the duty sergeant, the second she stepped through the main door.

Carla ran up the stairs in a quest to retrieve the evidence file Sara had left on her desk.

"In a cell. Want me to bring him through to an interview room?"

"Yes. What possessions did he have with him? A phone?"

"He did." The sergeant searched under the counter and removed an evidence bag.

Sara held out her hand. "I'll take that. It might help to influence him a little in there. What room shall we take?"

"Interview Room Two is free, ma'am."

Sara nodded, and with the phone in her hand, marched towards the room.

Carla joined her, holding the evidence file. "Let's hope he doesn't waste our time and gets on with it right away."

Sara sighed. "Wishful thinking on your part, but I think having this on the table next to us is bound to play a part in his decision-making." She held the phone up and then placed it on the desk.

The door opened a few minutes later, and a defiant-looking Richardson entered. He was cuffed already. The uniformed officer deposited him in the chair on the other side of the table and then took up his position at the back of the room. They glared at each other for the next five minutes until the duty solicitor joined them.

"Hello again, Miss Clarkson. Good of you to join us, especially on a Saturday."

"My pleasure as always, Inspector."

"Okay, Carla, can you get the proceedings underway for us?"

Carla started the recording machine. She announced the date and who the occupants were and added what the interview was regarding.

"Mr Richardson, perhaps you can tell us why you were holding Laura Tyler captive?"

He turned to his solicitor and grinned. "No comment."

Sara might have known that would be his response. She put her hand on top of his mobile. "Do you recognise this phone, Mr Richardson?"

"No comment."

"Okay, if that's how you want to play it. Let's see what evidence we have placing you at the scene, see if you can add a 'no comment' to the blindingly obvious facts." She opened the file and pushed across a photo of his car at the barn where they'd found Laura and also a picture taken in Sainsbury's car park. This was followed by another one of him passing by Andy Palmer's car.

Richardson stared and shrugged. "No comment."

"Here's the thing. This is the frame we're most interested in." She pushed another photo across the table and tapped a section of it with her finger. "In your hand you're carrying something. In this picture here, we can clearly see there's a piece of fabric matching the blouse that Laura was wearing when she was abducted and also when we found her this evening, where you were holding her."

"No comment."

"What I'm having trouble understanding is why you then walked past Andy Palmer's car and dropped the items you had in your hand in his boot."

His eyes narrowed. He shook his head slowly and grinned. "No comment."

"Okay, fair enough. At present, Laura Tyler is at the hospital. She'll be with us shortly. We'll put you in a line-up. I can guarantee she'll have no hesitation picking you out. You could make it so much easier on yourself if you simply tell us why you abducted her."

"No comment."

Sara picked up the phone. "Let's have a look at your contact list, shall we? Because it's my belief that you're in cahoots with someone. Or to put it another way, someone is yanking your strings, because I don't believe you'd have the intelligence to pull off something like this of your own volition. We're already checking into your bank account. No doubt that will throw up some interesting information for us soon enough."

He shrugged again. "No comment."

Sara tried to remain calm and resisted the temptation to reach across the table and slap the smarmy look off his face.

She opened the phone and tutted. "No password. Not advisable in this day and age, Mr Richardson."

She noted down a number in her notebook and slid it across to Carla. "Can you do me a favour? Check who this belongs to. It would appear that Mr Richardson has been in constant contact with this person since…oh, look, Tuesday of this week. Now, that might just be a coincidence, but I doubt it. Do you have anything to say about that, Mr Richardson?"

His shoulders sagged a little, and he appeared to sink deeper into his chair.

Carla left the room. Sara deliberately remained quiet, staring at Richardson, intimidating him, for the next five minutes until Carla returned.

"Can I see you outside, boss?"

Sara switched off the recording and joined her partner in the hallway. "Anything?"

"Yep, you're not going to believe who the number belongs to."

"Try me."

19

"How did we miss it?" Sara kept repeating over and over en route to the location.

"Will you stop blaming yourself? We had very little to go on as it was."

"We still missed it."

She cut the engine outside the house, and together they marched up to the front door. Carla rang the bell.

"Hello, Mr Tyler. Would it be possible to have a brief chat?"

"I've said all I had to say about Laura. Wait, have you found her?"

A movement over his shoulder caught Sara's eye. "We'll reveal all once you let us in."

He took a step back and motioned for them to enter. "Gillian, can you put the kettle on?"

"That won't be necessary. Perhaps you and your wife would like to join us in the living room?" Sara led the way, followed by a stunned Mr and Mrs Tyler.

Carla entered the room behind them and closed the door.

"Well, have you found her?" Bobby insisted, leaning against the mantelpiece.

"As it happens, yes, we have. Which is why we're here, to ask you both some further questions."

He frowned. "Like what? What does this have to do with us?"

Sara's gaze drifted over to Gillian who was shifting uncomfortably in her seat. "Perhaps your wife would like to fill in the gaps for us. Gillian?"

"What?" she shrieked, her gaze darting between the three of them.

"Perhaps you can tell us why your phone number was found on the abductor's mobile? Not only that, we've searched the abductor's bank details and stumbled across two payments amounting to five thousand two hundred pounds, transferred from your account. These payments were made this week, since Tuesday, in fact, the day Laura went missing."

"What's she saying, Gillian? That you were behind this?"

Gillian's lip turned up at the side, and she nodded. "Yes, it was me. I had every intention of teaching her a lesson she wouldn't forget."

"By starving her to death?" Sara bit back.

"It wouldn't have come to that."

Bobby placed his clenched fist to his forehead. "Jesus Christ, this is bloody insane. Why? Why would you do such a thing?"

"Because you still love her..." Gillian's voice trailed off.

"Are you bloody kidding me? I don't. When have I ever given you that impression? It's you I love, no one else. How can you think that, after what that woman did to me?"

"I sat there, listening to you. You were cut up about her not speaking to you when you saw her recently. It started the ball rolling. I know how devastated you were about what she did to you. You also told me the lies she'd told about her father...and, well, I took it upon myself to punish her."

"Why now? After all these years?" Bobby demanded, his cheeks flaming with rage.

"It's been eating away at me. The last straw came when she ignored you recently. The callous bitch, after everything you had to put up with. How dare she treat you and the others in her life that way?"

Bobby growled. "Really? And you think what you've done to her makes you any better than her? You crazy bitch! How dare you mess with people's lives and their heads like that? You're far worse than her, if you're capable of setting something like this up. What the fuck? Who the fuck am I married to? Please, someone tell me, because I'll be bloody damned if I know. Jesus on a frigging bike, it comes to something when you have no idea of the warped thoughts your other half is having while they're lying in bed with you at night. You're sick…just get her out of my sight, will you, Inspector?"

Sara stepped forward, her cuffs in her hand.

Gillian lashed out and then dropped to the deep-pile carpet at her feet. "No, you can't do this. I did it for you, Bobby, you're my life, my heart, my soul. Please don't let them take me away."

"What? You're unbelievable." He surged forward and grabbed her arm, tried to yank her to her feet, but Carla unlatched his hand and stood between them. "Just get her out of my house. If you don't, you could have a murder inquiry on your hands."

"Noooo…please, don't do this, Bobby. I love you…I did this for you, to show you how deep my love is for you."

Exasperated, Bobby stared at Sara and shouted, "Get her out. *Now*."

"All right. We're going. I'll need you to come down the station to give us a statement. Monday will do."

"I'll do it. Make sure you bloody throw the book at that bitch. I want nothing more to do with her. Shit, with her crazy mind, I suppose I have to count myself lucky she hasn't knifed me in my sleep over the years."

Sara and Carla hauled Gillian to her feet—she refused to stand. They ended up dragging her out of the house and into the car. All the while, she glanced back at her husband, pleading with him to forgive her.

"Forgive you…?" he shouted. "The bloody universe would have to come to an abrupt halt before I did that."

EPILOGUE

*D*espite the late hour, Sara insisted that she and the team celebrate their success at the pub around the corner from the station. Sara smiled when Carol Price joined the group at around nine p.m.

"How's Laura?" Sara asked, eager to hear the news.

"She's going to be okay. Thankfully, there's been no lasting damage to her internal organs. Everything is functioning as it should be. They're going to keep her in for a few days, just to make sure."

"Aww, that's the best news I've had all day. We arrested the ex-husband's wife. She was behind the abduction."

The chief scratched her head. "Seriously? Why?"

"Payback for the way Laura treated Bobby."

"That's insane, after all this time?"

"Yep. It was triggered when Laura ignored Bobby a little while back. You know what? It's too bizarre for words. People need to take a good look at themselves before they judge others."

"Ain't that the truth? Anyway, I couldn't miss out on the celebrations. This isn't the first time I've said this, and I doubt it's going to be the last either, you guys are amazing. I can't thank you enough. Having heard the lies Laura has told over the years and the damage they caused her character, I have to admire your professionalism in dealing with the case. You never gave up. I'll forever be in your debt." She ended her speech with tears in her eyes.

Sara's throat clogged up. She raised her glass. "To the best team ever to grace Hereford."

The team all cheered and sipped their drinks.

"Well, I suppose I'd better get home to my man. He'll think I've run out on him." Sara chuckled.

"He's got a good 'un in you, Sara Ramsey. I wonder if he realises how lucky he is."

"He does. I make a point of reminding him every day. Enjoy the rest of your weekend, guys. Skeleton staff tomorrow. Craig, Barry, if any cases come in needing my input, delay ringing me until Monday. I have a wedding to plan tomorrow."

THE END

KEEP IN TOUCH WITH THE AUTHOR

Newsletter
http://smarturl.it/8jtcvv

BookBub
www.bookbub.com/authors/m-a-comley

Blog
http://melcomley.blogspot.com

Join my special Facebook group to take part in monthly giveaways.

Readers' Group

A NOTE TO YOU, THE READER

Dear Reader,

What a twisted read that was.
But as usual, Sara and her team came to the rescue in her own inimitable way. An intriguing tale nevertheless, I'm sure you'll agree.
Sara will be back again soon with another fast-paced thriller.
In the meantime, perhaps you'll consider reading one of my other thriller series? Have you tried the bestselling, award-winning Justice series yet?
Here's the link to the first book in this gripping thriller series <u>CRUEL JUSTICE</u>

Thank you for your support as always. If you could find it in your heart to leave a review, I'd be eternally grateful, they're like nectar from the Gods to authors.

M A Comley

Printed in Great Britain
by Amazon